THE BLACK
ALABASTER BOX

THE BLACK ALABASTER BOX

FRANCES SCHOONMAKER

The Last Crystal Trilogy, book 1

Illustrated by the author

Auctus Publishers
Havertown, Pennsylvania, United States

Auctus Publishers
606 Merion Ave, First Floor
Havertown, PA 19083, USA

Softcover ISBN 978-0-9979607-4-7
Hardcover ISBN 978-0-9979607-5-4
Electronic ISBN 978-0-9979607-6-1

Library of Congress Control Number: 2018936008

for Amelia
junior editor and co-conspirator

ACKNOWLEDGMENTS

Liesl Bolin, you have been a support, assistant, and adviser from the beginning. (Every writer should have an English-Theatre graduate in the family.) Warren Schoonmaker, I appreciate your understanding of First Nations People, knowledge of geology, the American West, and our many conversations about plot. (You are a better brother than Junior Swathmore.) Isaiah Laich and Sarah VanTiem, your reading of the first draft and feedback were more important than you can imagine. (Isaiah, there are some things only a child can do.) Thank you, Katie Schmidt for sharing and critiquing the draft with your fifth graders at Rodgers Forge Elementary School. Girls and Boys, I enjoyed meeting and talking with you: Jackson B., Eve B., Rea B. Natasha B., Amelia B., Audrey B., Mackenzie C., Xavier C., Sam C., Zach D., Abigail D., Owen G., Alex H., Colin K., Mary L., Griffen M., Ruby M., Colin M., Elise N., Ava O., Fisher P., Malena R., Grey R., Dillan R., Caroline S., Alejandro V., and Madison W. (It turns out that a book about a random girl going West, written by somebody's grandmother can keep you clamoring for the next chapter.) Jon Dunlap, your support in reading The Last Crystal and sharing The Black Alabaster Box with your fourth and fifth graders at Rivendell School was enormously helpful. Thanks to your class for their thoughtful critique (I'm glad they are eager for the next book). And thanks, Tanya Sherman for convincing Mona to pose for the cover and helping to make it happen.

CONTENTS

Chapter 1

OLD SHEP RETURNS

Grace Willis stood at the front door looking out, wondering what it would be like tomorrow when she no longer had a home. *Will the robins nest in the lilac bushes this spring without me to watch over them? Who will collect seed pods when the Catalpa trees drop them along the driveway? Will the garden know I am gone?* She was utterly miserable.

Left up to her, nothing would change. But Grace didn't get to choose. With new land opening in the West, her father and mother were determined to go to California. It was their dream to start a medical school. *So tomorrow is the auction. And there is nothing I can do about it.* Grace heaved a great sigh.

Just then, a big black and white dog came bounding up the front porch steps. Wagging all over, the dog looked at her as if they were best friends and he was asking permission to come over and play.

"It's Old Shep!" Grace called, momentarily distracted from her misery.

"Why, he does look just like Old Shep," said Daddy.

"It can't be," said Mamma, joining them at the door. "Old Shep would be at least one hundred three in dog years by now. Dogs don't live that long."

Looking at Daddy, the dog held up his right paw. Daddy stepped out on the porch. Shaking the paw respectfully, he asked, "Do you mind if I have a look, old fellow? You all can come out, he's a gentle dog."

The dog sat quietly. Daddy knelt beside him, carefully feeling the paw and all the way up the leg. "Apparently this dog does live that long," he said. "This is Old Shep. His leg healed nicely, if I do say so."

"Really, you can't be Old Shep," Mamma said kindly as she sat down in a rocking chair. The dog went to her, putting his head in her lap. "Why, you are Old Shep!" Mamma exclaimed. "Remember how he used to do that? I'll swear, you don't look a day older."

"Perhaps we misjudged his age," said Daddy. Sitting down on the porch swing, he motioned for Grace to sit beside him.

"Either that or he's magic!" Mamma scratched Old Shep behind the ears.

"I'm not entirely prepared to rule out magic," said Daddy, giving Mamma a knowing look. "There are plenty of things in this world that can't be explained."

Dogs aren't magic, thought Grace. *But, if he was magic, I'd tell him to stop the auction from happening.*

"Old Shep had a broken leg when a friend left him with us, Grace," Daddy explained. "You probably don't remember Mr. C'lestin. You were a little tot then. Old Shep was limping and in a lot of pain. I set his leg. He stayed with us almost a year. Then he just disappeared. That was nearly ten years ago."

"Mr. C'lestin didn't come for him?" asked Grace.

"I daresay he had his reasons," said Daddy. "C'lestin is an unusual person, a bit mysterious—but very nice."

"Old Shep must not have been his dog," concluded Grace. "But why didn't Old Shep want to be our dog? We loved him."

"I'm not so sure you can say that Old Shep *belongs* to anyone," said Daddy carefully, searching for the right word. "It is more like we became part of his circle of friends. Now he's come back to see us."

"I smell dinner," exclaimed Mamma. "It's our last dinner in this house. I'd sure hate for it to burn. Come set the table, Grace."

Last dinner. Reluctantly, Grace washed her hands at the kitchen pump and set the table.

She could have stayed with Grandpa and Grandma Willis the next day while the auction went on, but she refused to go. In one last effort to bring things to a halt, she dug her heels in and had an all out, screaming tantrum. But it didn't do any good.

"I know this is hard, Grace," said Mama, sighing. "You are going to have to decide if you are a part of this and ready to accept an adventure, or if you're going to cling to your misery and lock out the world. Either way, we are going to California and so are you."

Old Shep stayed by her side the whole terrible day. He was the only one who acted like he understood how she felt. When she crawled under the porch, he went with her. When she retreated to the carriage house in the back yard, he came along. When she hid in her secret place in the bushes behind the Catalpa trees, he was there.

They watched from her hiding places as strangers hauled off one precious thing after another. By the end of the day the house was completely empty. It was no longer their house. Somebody bought it, too.

After the auction, they stayed with Grandpa and Grandma Willis. All too soon family and friends came to help them load their wagon.

"That's a real fine thing you and the Mrs. are doing, Doc," said one of their neighbors as they stacked supplies on the wagon. "I wouldn't have the courage to go West."

"You sure do have a lot of books and medical supplies piled up in there," said one of the men as they finished loading. "You might ought to take more food. It's a long ways out there from what I hear. You can't eat books!"

Daddy good-naturedly shook the man's hand. "You're right, Paul. Don't worry. We'll be trading for a bigger wagon once we get to Kansas City. We'll stock up on provisions there."

"I reckon they don't have good doctors way out there in California," said an uncle. "Still, we sure will miss you all."

"Amen to that. We'll miss having the best doctor in St. Louis right next door!" said one of the women, giving Mamma a hug. "Lord knows I'll miss you, Amanda. And little Grace, too," she added, wiping away tears.

Little? Grace was offended, but she didn't say anything. Mamma would say back talk is rude.

Grandpa and Grandma Rhoads lived on a farm way out in the country. They stayed over at the Willis house to see them off the next morning. The sun was barely up when their last good-byes were said. Grandma Willis gave Grace a whole tin of gingerbread men. "These won't last you all the way to California. When you get settled out there, I'll just have to send you some more." There were tears in her eyes. Grace gave her a hug. There were tears in her eyes, too.

Grandma Rhoads held her close. "I know you don't have room for another thing, but I want you to have this, Grace. I made it for you. It won't take up much room. When you hold it, just remember how much you are loved. Two thousand miles can't change that." She gave her a linen handkerchief with a wide crochet lace border. It was beautiful, but when Grace thought of all the things she wished she could take, she hadn't thought of handkerchiefs. She thanked Grandma and hugged her just the same. She didn't want to hurt her feelings.

"Reckon you're takin' that dog," said Grandpa Willis. Old Shep stood waiting by the horses.

"Leastwise he seems to think so," said Grandpa Rhoads, chuckling.

"Old Shep makes his own decisions," said Daddy. He laughed, but there were tears in his eyes as he got in the wagon where Grace and Mamma now waited. Mamma wiped her eyes.

How can they be happy and sad at the same time? Grace wondered. All she could feel was sadness. Tears made their way down her face and splashed on her hands.

Then came the moment Grace dreaded most of all. They set off for the frontier town of Kansas City. Behind her, fading into the distance was all she had ever known and just about everybody she loved. She had lived in the big house in St. Louis, Missouri her whole safe, comfortable, uneventful life.

Chapter 2

DO YOU BELIEVE IN MAGIC?

It took almost two weeks to get to Kansas City. Once there, they met up with Bill Stokes, a Wagon Master who knew the Santa Fe Trail and how to run a wagon train. They traded their wagon in on a bigger wagon with a canvas bonnet. They bought a milk cow, a team of six oxen, and a whole bunch of supplies like corn flour, salt pork, dried beans, and dried apples.

Things happened around Grace with blinding speed. Mamma and Daddy were happy and filled with excitement over the trip. "It's a dream coming true," Mamma said. But Grace felt as if she were watching from somewhere outside herself. She clung to Old Shep like an island in the sea. Try as she would, she could not enjoy the adventure going on around her. Every new thing made her want to go home again.

She spent almost all of her free time under the wagon with Old Shep, trying to figure out what she would have to do to convince her parents to go back to St. Louis. She was sitting there alone one afternoon with the tin of gingerbread men, trying to decide how to ration them. She was afraid that when they were all gone a piece of Grandma Willis would be gone, too. Old Shep, usually by her side, had gone with Daddy into the town.

A scruffy-looking girl stuck her head under the wagon. Right behind her was an even scruffier-looking boy. Grace hadn't met them, but new families joined the Stokes Company every day. The pair looked to be about her age. Grace wondered if they would be friends.

"This here is Junior," said the girl, grinning, "we seen you crawl under here."

"My name is Grace Willis, what's yours?"

"Ruby Swathmore. Junior knows magic, don't ya, Junior."

"Yeah," said Junior, snickering. He wiped his nose on his sleeve.

"Want to see some magic?" asked Ruby. "Junior can make stuff disappear."

"Sure," said Grace.

"Close your eyes," said Ruby.

The minute she closed her eyes, Junior grabbed the cookie tin, crawling out from under the wagon in a flash. Ruby was right after him. "You better give me my share, Junior. I'll knock the snot out of you if you don't."

Grace followed them, too furious to think about what she'd do if she actually caught up. They raced across the field where wagons were collecting, dodging in and out among them. Then they let her catch up, making no effort to hide. "Told ya he could make stuff disappear," taunted Ruby, turning to face her. Her mouth was so full of gingerbread she could hardly talk. "I can make stuff disappear, too. Specially gingerbread." A great glob of gingerbread showed as she talked.

"That was mean," Grace said, trying to stand her ground. "I would have shared."

"Yeah? Want to make somethin' of it?" asked Junior, talking with his mouth full. The empty tin was on the ground where he'd dropped it. They had stuffed every last bit of gingerbread into their mouths.

There wasn't any use trying to talk and Grace wasn't a fighter. Besides, there were two of them, both a good inch taller than she was. She picked up the tin, tears of anger burning in her eyes, and walked away.

Mamma listened sympathetically. "I'm so sorry," she said.

"They ate every last gingerbread. Every last one. All I have is this one," Grace sobbed, pulling it from her pocket. "Grandma made them especially for me. And I was stupid enough to close my eyes."

"Don't be too hard on yourself," said Mamma, putting her arms around Grace. "It would have been good fun if he had been magic, wouldn't it? You were right to walk away, though. Maybe you should just try to stay away from them."

"I don't believe in magic anyway," said Grace.

"You don't?" Mamma asked. "What a dull world it would be without magic in it. How uninteresting if nothing extraordinary ever happened."

"Why can't we go home?" Grace whined. It didn't do any good. It never did.

"But we are home," said Mamma. "Home is where we are all together." She always said that. Grace quit listening before Mamma got to the part about looking forward and how she'd miss out on all the fun if she kept looking backward.

The evening the Johnson wagon arrived, everything changed. Grace and Old Shep stood watching as a new wagon pulled up. *Twenty-one*, she counted to herself. *Mr. Stokes says we have to have thirty wagons before we can leave. Why do they keep coming?*

Chapter 2

A boy stuck his head out from the canvas bonnet. "Oh! Ha-llo there," he said. There was something about the way he said it and the mischief in his eyes that told her they were going to be friends.

It was early the next morning when they actually met. The field where wagons were collecting for the journey west was full of wild flowers and tall prairie grass. Grace grudgingly admitted to herself that it was beautiful in the early morning with dew sparkling from every leaf and wild-flower.

She and Old Shep were out before breakfast gathering flowers when she saw Ruby and Junior. Laughing gleefully, they poked at something with a stick. She was about to turn and walk in the opposite direction when a rough looking man stepped into view. "What's the big idea of you two runnin' off like that?" he yelled. "Get back here before I have to take off my belt." Dropping their stick, Ruby and Junior fled back to their wagon. Grace couldn't help smiling. *Serves them right.*

Curious about what they had been doing, Grace waited until Ruby and Junior were out of sight. An ant den stood in a bare place in the tall grass. Right on top of it was a little creature no bigger than the back of her hand. She couldn't tell if it was a lizard or some kind of frog. It was reddish brown with dark spots and spikey all over. Two spikes stuck out from the back of its head like a little collar. The poor thing was covered in patches of blood. Ruby and Junior must have hurt it.

Grace didn't know what to do. She couldn't stand to see it suffer, but she was afraid to pick it up.

Just then Sid appeared. He carried a long stick, using it as a walking staff. Following him were a much younger boy and girl. They carried long sticks, too.

"What cha found?" Sid asked.

"I don't know," said Grace. "Some kind of creature. I think Ruby and Junior hurt it. They may have put it on the ant den to see if the ants would eat it." Then, noticing his quizical look, she added, "Ruby and Junior are two big bullies."

Sid leaned over to look. "Why that's nothin' but a horned toad," he said.

"It's wounded," said Grace.

"No, somethin' must 'a upset it, maybe it was them pokin' at it," said Sid. "Look how puffed up he is. They do that to protect themselves. Don't worry about the ants. He's glad to be on an ant den." He straightened up, putting an arm over the little girl's shoulder as she and the boy gathered around. "Ya see, horned toads like to eat ants. They sit by an ant den and gobble them up as they walk past. The ants can crawl all over him and it doesn't hurt him one bit."

"But he's bleeding," pleaded Grace, still worried. "Ruby and Junior must have hurt him."

"Maybe not. I reckon they was tryin' to get him upset. If he's frightened, a horned toad can squirt blood from the corner of his eye. It's a weapon that keeps skunks and coyotes and bigger animals like that from havin' him for breakfast. Horned toads won't hurt you. I wouldn't pick up one that's sittin' on an ant den, though. You might get stung even if he doesn't."

"I saw your wagon come in last night," said Grace. "My name's Grace Willis, what's yours?"

"Sid Johnson. This is my little brother Jimmy and my sister Cora. Mamma asked me to take them for a walk before breakfast. She wants us out of her hair while she's settin' up camp."

"We're explorers," said Jimmy, standing just a bit taller and gripping his walking stick.

Cora took her thumb out of her mouth long enough to say, "I'm a 'splorer, too."

"Oh good," said Grace. "Maybe we can all be explorers together."

"You have to have a walkin' stick," said Jimmy.

Sid grinned. "It's okay Jimmy. We'll find her one." He had such a carefree, easy manner. Grace envied him.

"Can I pat your dog?" asked Jimmy.

Old Shep, who had stayed back all this time, stepped forward, wagging his tail as if he knew exactly what was called for.

"Sure," said Grace, trying to sound casual and carefree like Sid.

"Let him smell your hand first," advised Sid. He held out his hand to Old Shep, who sniffed it approvingly. Cora didn't wait. Dropping her stick and taking her thumb from her mouth, she threw her arms around the dog in a big hug. Old Shep stood patiently, tail wagging.

With Sid as a friend, Grace quit thinking so much about going home. They always found interesting things to do when they weren't busy with chores. They explored under every wagon as new families joined the train. Sometimes it was the two of them and Old Shep. Sometimes Jimmy and Cora came along. Sometimes other kids from the camp joined them.

By the time the wagon train pulled out of Kansas City, the younger children in the train counted on them to organize games of hide and seek, hopscotch, cat's cradle, or marbles. With Sid as her ally, Grace didn't worry about Ruby and Junior. Sid wasn't any bigger than the twins. In fact he wasn't quite as tall as Junior. He wasn't a bully either. But something in his manner said, *Don't even try.*

One day they were walking beside the Willis wagon, trying to stay in the shade cast by the canvas bonnet. "Do you believe in magic, Sid?" Grace asked.

"Sure," said Sid in his matter-of-fact, casual way. "Don't you?"

"I don't know," said Grace doubtfully. Then she told him how Old Shep showed up on the porch the day before the auction.

"One hundred three in dog years," repeated Sid thoughtfully. "Why couldn't he be? Old Shep is no ordinary dog, I'll tell you that much."

"What do you mean?" asked Grace, bewildered. "He doesn't do spells or turn people into frogs or anything. And he sure didn't stop the auction from happening."

"That's not magic. That's fairy tales," said Sid. "There's somethin' about Old Shep. He understands stuff. He's wise. Maybe he is one hundred three. Maybe he's a whole lot older."

"But what good is it?" Grace persisted.

"I don't know. Maybe it doesn't have to be any good. Maybe it just is. Race you to the front of the train." Sid was off in a leap, Old Shep bounding after him. Grace ran, her bonnet falling off her head and dangling behind her, wind whipping through her hair.

Chapter 3

TROUBLING NEWS

They hadn't been on the trail more than a couple of weeks, when Grace overheard something troubling. It was past bedtime. She was supposed to be fast asleep. Snatches of conversation drifted her way as the men talked in low voices.

"They say traffic along the California Road is easin' up." It was Bill Stokes. She liked Mr. Stokes. He was a firm leader, but there was a twinkle in his eye. That twinkle counted for a lot.

"Reckon they done hauled all the gold out of California by now," Grace didn't recognize this voice.

"Is that the trail that follows the Canadian River?" somebody asked.

"They say the Canadian cuts all the way from Western Oklahoma through Texas," said somebody else. "Anybody know where it ends?"

The men talked like that every night. She yawned.

"Wasn't Josiah Greg the one who followed the Canadian to Santa Fe, New Mexico? Leastwise he cut through Oklahoma Territory into Comanche lands," said Mr. Stokes. Grace yawned again and rolled over.

"Josiah Greg went on good luck and a prayer," said Jim Payne. "The army sent Nathan Boone's party along that same stretch. Boone's party opened it up for wagon traffic." Grace liked Jim Payne, too. Sometimes he scouted for the wagon train, riding out to see what was ahead. He was a kind man, never too busy to say hello, even to a young girl. Before the wagon train set out from Kansas City, the men elected a Wagon Captain. Daddy thought Jim Payne would be good. But some of the men didn't feel right voting for a Free Negro. They elected Ben Johnson, Sid's Daddy. Grace was glad for Sid, but she couldn't understand why the men didn't feel right about Mr. Payne. Daddy said some things were hard to understand, even for grown-ups, and he hoped it would be different in California.

"Well, Jim, reckon that's what we all count on," Mr. Stokes laughed, "good luck and a prayer." The men joined in the laughter good-naturedly.

Their wagon train was smaller than most of those that followed the Santa Fe Trail. Most wagon trains carried trade goods. They went in large groups, sometimes several hundred at a time for protection from American Indians and gangs of outlaws. But it had been quiet all along the Santa Fe Trail for more than a year. A few wagon trains like theirs preferred the Santa Fe to the southern route west. Like the Stokes Company, these trains were smaller than the commercial wagon trains and made up of families looking to settle in California.

Hiram Swathmore spoke up. "I'll wager there's still money to be made along that there California Road." Grace recognized his wheedling voice. It gave her a chill. "A body could set up a tradin' post. Trade with Injuns and folk goin' West."

"It would take more courage than I've got!" Ben Johnson said. "Safe when you have a small army at your back is one thing. Safe for the likes of you and me is another. You'd be a sittin' duck in the middle of nowhere, Hiram." Grace liked the Johnson family. Like Sid, they were all sensible, but they were lively and full of fun, too.

"Anyways, there's money to be made trappin'," said Mr. Swathmore.

That man scares the daylights out of me, Grace thought. She was wide-awake now.

"What are you goin' to trap on the Canadian River, Hiram?" called one of the men. "Sand rats? That's all desert from what I've heard." Laughter broke out all around.

Voices began to fade. The men were returning to their own wagons for the night.

Then came the troubling part. "I'll look in on the boy again in the morning, Ben." Grace sat up. Her father was talking. "Get me up if anything changes in the night."

"The Misses says Sid's been runnin' a high fever since afternoon," said Mr. Johnson. "I don't know what to think, Doc. I'm scared."

"I know, Ben. I know," said her father. "Let's take one step at a time."

Grace wanted to stick her head out of the wagon and ask Daddy what it was all about, but she was supposed to be asleep. Besides, he didn't always tell her things she wanted to know.

She usually played with Sid in the late afternoon when it wasn't too hot. Sometimes they ran to the front of the train, then walked backwards, letting the wagons pass until the Johnson wagon or the Willis wagon caught up. Sid hadn't been out this afternoon. Mrs. Johnson said he was asleep. It wasn't like Sid.

"What do you think, Doc?" It was Bill Stokes talking in a low voice.

"Like I told Ben, we have to wait and see," said her father.

"This is the second wagon," Mr. Stokes sounded grim. "You know as well as I do, if the Johnson boy has smallpox we're in trouble. The pox could wipe out the whole train in a matter of weeks."

"Look, Bill, if we can get people to coop-erate, we should be able keep it from spreading," said Daddy.

"That's what I try to tell folk from the get-go," said Mr. Stokes. "Wagon trains are more at risk from disease than from Indian attack. People waste their time worrying about Indians. They should be worrying about things like small pox and cholera. That's the honest truth of it."

Their voices died away. Worried, Grace tossed and turned until at last she fell into a trou-bled asleep. For the first time since she'd met Sid, she dreamed of her room at home with its four-poster featherbed and the flower garden quilt made by Grandma Rhoads.

Somebody was crying when she awoke just before dawn. Her mother stood outside the wagon, wrapped in a shawl, with an arm around Sadie Johnson, Sid's mother.

"His face and arms was broke out this mornin'," wept Mrs. Johnson.

Chapter 3

The wagon belonging to the Johnson family pulled away from the close circle of wagons. Nobody had to say the dreaded words for Grace to know. Sid Johnson had smallpox.

"What will happen to them, Mamma?" Grace asked, fighting to hold back tears.

"Your Daddy's taking care of Sid," said Mamma, giving her a good morning kiss. "All we can do is pray." She spoke calmly, but she looked worried.

Grace shivered. She wondered if there were more to the story. Her parents didn't tell her things they thought would worry her. But she heard things. She knew more than they thought she knew. Jimmy and little Cora were complaining of headache and back pain, meaning that they'd probably been infected. What was going to happen to them? And what was going to happen to the wagon train? She wished they could go home.

Chapter 4

HARD WORDS

With morning's first light, everyone was up and about. Women and girls hurriedly made breakfast. Men and boys rounded up the oxen, hitched up the teams, and got wagons into line. Everything had to be ready for the train to leave by seven o'clock sharp.

"Where's Daddy?" Grace asked, climbing down from the wagon to help with breakfast.

"He's already with the Johnsons. He'll stay with them until they are settled and know what to do. Then he'll catch up with the train." Mamma said.

"We'll be far away by then," said Grace fearfully.

"He'll be on horse back," Mamma reassured her, "he won't have any trouble catching up."

Chapter 4

"Where's Old Shep?" asked Grace, looking around.

"He is with your Daddy. Sadie Johnsons says he slept under their wagon last night. Mr. Stokes is hitching up our team. You and I will drive. What do you think about that?" Mamma made everything sound like an adventure.

"Better he should stay here and protect the rest of us," said Mrs. Swathmore, who was sharing their campfire. She always talked in an irritating, whiny little girl voice. Grace had never met anybody so disagreeable.

Every day, Bill Stokes ordered the thirty wagons in their train to take a different position in line. Grace dreaded it when the time came for the Swathmore wagon to go before or after their wagon. Mrs. Swathmore never made her own campfire. She constantly handed over her baby to somebody else to hold and did as little work as possible. In fact, the only thing she seemed to do was complain in that high-pitched whine of hers.

The twins, Ruby and Junior, constantly made trouble. Stealing Grace's cookies was just the beginning. They delighted in torturing their brother and sister, five-year-old Otis and three-year-old Myrtle. Grace and Sid steered clear of the twins, who never touched Sid. But they had a way of shoving or pinching Grace, then blaming it on somebody else. They were sore losers, too, so they constantly spoiled games for everybody.

Mamma was patient with them when the Swathmores shared the campfire. She always had an encouraging word for the twins. She promised them extra bits of salt pork, cornbread, or biscuits as a reward if they washed up before mealtime and said please and thank-you. Mrs. Swathmore said washing up was a waste of good water. But since Mamma provided the water from the Willis barrel, she didn't refuse.

The twins were glad to have anything Mamma cooked. Mrs. Swathmore usually served up greasy corncakes, burned on the outside and not quite cooked on the inside. Everything she cooked was thrown together half-heartedly. It felt like even her cooking was a way of whining.

At night, after the camp chores were all done, people gathered around a campfire and sang songs or told stories. Even Ruby and Junior sat still for a story. It was the only time Grace dared sit next to them.

As the company broke camp that morning, Bill Stokes gave orders for the day. "You all know the Johnson wagon pulled out of the circle early this mornin'. Sid Johnson has smallpox. Doc Willis and Jim Payne are stayin' behind to help them get settled. When they're on their feet again, the Johnsons will join up with another train comin' this way. Meanwhile, if anybody comes down with a fever, report it to me immediately. Doc Willis says that if we take proper precautions, we should be able to control an outbreak.

We're lucky to have the Willis wagon with us. Not every wagon train headed to California has a doctor along." He went over a list of things they had to do—hand washing was one of them.

"Grace, dear, why don't you take your doll to the wagon and get her settled for travel," said Mamma. Grace knew that she was being sent to the wagon so she wouldn't hear all the grown-up talk that was bound to follow the announcement.

This was one of those times Grace didn't obey. She didn't intend to eavesdrop, but she told herself she couldn't help hearing. Besides, if anything was being said about Sid, she had a right to know.

Not surprisingly, Mr. Swathmore spoke up. His scarred face said that he had nothing to fear from an outbreak of smallpox. He'd already had it sometime in the past, so he was unlikely to be in any danger. "Be a shame to lose the goods in the Johnson wagon if they all die. Like as not the rest of 'em will be down before the day's out. Better leave 'em to themselves and divide up their goods with those as can use 'em."

Grace caught her breath. Were the Johnsons really going to die?

"That would be inhumane!" scolded one of the women.

"You could leave 'em some food and water," said a man who didn't seem to think it was such a bad idea.

"If they're going to die anyway," said another.

"Is that the way you'd want to be treated if it was any of you left back?" It sounded like Jim Payne's wife. Grace liked her, too. She was a schoolteacher somewhere up North before she married Mr. Payne. Sometimes at night she'd hear lessons with the children who wanted to sit with her and recite. Grace and Sid never missed an opportunity.

"I don't reckon they'll care one way or another," scoffed Mr. Swathmore, "not if they're dead."

"Shame on all of you!" scolded Mrs. Payne. "Who said they're going to die?"

Angry grumbling broke out. Dropping all pretense of obeying her mother, Grace stuck her head out of the wagon canvas to see what was going on.

"You ought to have stayed back with the Johnsons, Swathmore," yelled one of the men. "You and Doc Willis are the only ones safe from the pox."

Like Mr. Swathmore, Grace's father had nothing to fear from smallpox. As a boy he, too, had survived a mild case of the disease, though his face was less marked than was Mr. Swathmore's.

Mr. Swathmore spat a stream of chewing tobacco on the ground at his feet. "Got a family to take care of," he said.

Chapter 4

"And Jim Payne doesn't?" called another man.

With that, Bill Stokes put an end to the talk. "In Ben Johnson's absence, Quinton Davis will act as Captain until we can have an election. Now lets get this company on the trail. We don't have time to stand around jawing. We've got miles to cover." Then he added, "There will be no more talk of abandoning anybody as long as I'm your Wagon Master. Everyone will take a turn if we need people to stay behind and help a family in their time of need. It's in the by-laws you adopted before we set out."

"Not me," muttered Mr. Swathmore. "I ain't stayin' behind to watch over somebody who is goinna' die anyway. For my part we shouldn't be wastin' money on some uppity Wagon Master, either." Tobacco juice drooled out of the side of his mouth. He wiped it on his sleeve.

Mrs. Swathmore stood next to him, holding their baby. "Why can't we go back?" she whined. "Trail life is too hard on my nerves. You don't know how I suffer. I can't last all the way to California without someone to do the chores. It ain't right."

"I've a mind to split off and go south to Oklahoma Territory anyways," Mr. Swathmore muttered. "I hear there's good land and money to be made on the California Road. Might be able to pick up some goods on the way, if you get my meaning. Build up our reserves. There's goina' be some as don't need 'em." He gave Mrs. Swathmore a sly look, "better to split off than have you and the youngins gettin' the pox anyways."

Grace shuddered, pulling her head back into the wagon. She had a feeling he meant to steal from the Johnson wagon if he could. She was terrified of Mr. Swathmore. She hoped they would leave and go south. But she didn't want him to steal from the Johnsons. She wanted Sid to get well and rejoin the wagon train. *Except Mr. Stokes said the Johnsons will join another train when everybody gets well—if they get well.* She already missed Sid. He was more fun than anybody. Besides, he was the only one who could stand up to Ruby and Junior. *What will I do without Sid?* Grace had an awful feeling in the pit of her stomach. She blinked hard to keep from crying. Now, more than ever, she wanted to go home.

Chapter 5

GOING ON

As the wagons began to get in line for the day, Mamma said Grace could pick some wild-flowers for Sid. She was under strict orders to give them to Daddy and get back before the train pulled out. She found white anemone, purple phlox, and yellow primroses not far from the trail. They made a cheerful posy. Grace didn't feel cheerful. Worry hung over her like a dark cloud as she handed the flowers to Daddy and told him goodbye. Then she hugged Old Shep, who was standing by the Johnson wagon. "Old Shep, if you are magic, don't let him die," she whispered.

It was two days later while they were setting up camp for the night when Daddy and Jim Payne caught up with the wagon train. Old Shep trotted behind. Grace could tell from their faces that they brought the worst possible news. Sid

Johnson was dead. But it looked like Jimmy and Cora were going to have a much milder case. It was too early to tell about Mr. and Mrs. Johnson. They would know by the time the next train came along. Meanwhile, the Johnsons knew exactly what to do to take care of themselves.

The news hit Grace like a hard punch in the stomach. She had never known anybody her own age to die. Sid was her best friend. *I didn't even get to tell him goodbye.* When they left St. Louis for the Santa Fe Trail, Grace thought that leaving home was the worst thing that could ever happen to a girl. Losing Sid was far worse. She crawled under the wagon. Burying her face in Old Shep, she cried. *How could you let this happen, Old Shep? If you really were magic, you wouldn't have let him die.* She cried until she fell into an exhausted sleep. She didn't wake up until she heard Mamma calling, "Oh, there you are! Don't you want something for supper, darling?"

Mamma had a way of knowing what was hurting. She crawled under the wagon and put her arms around Grace, holding her. "I'm so sorry, sweetheart. I know you'll miss Sid. He was such a good friend for you. Sometimes things don't turn out right. I wish I could change that."

"But why?" Grace demanded. "Why did it have to be Sid?"

"I don't know," said Mamma. There were tears in her eyes. "There are some questions that don't have answers." They crawled out from under the wagon.

Daddy put his big, comforting hand on her shoulder. "I'm sorry Grace. It's a terrible thing to lose a friend. That's why we're going to California, so we can learn more about diseases and keep good people like Sid Johnson from dying."

"Then I wish we were in California now," said Grace, tears streaming again, "if we have to go." It wouldn't help Sid anyway.

After that Daddy and Mamma worked day and night helping families in the wagon train. When anybody had a fever, one of them was there to help. Mamma wasn't a doctor, but she had worked with Daddy long enough to know a great deal about how to take care of people. Sometimes one of the other adults drove the Willis wagon so Mamma and Daddy were free to sit with others who needed them. Most of the time, things weren't serious. Members of the wagon train took her daddy seriously when he said they had to follow the rules for preventing the spread of smallpox. But still it spread.

One awful night, Mamma fainted as she was cooking dinner. Grace ran to her. Daddy got there first. He caught Mamma before she hit the ground. "She has a high fever," he said.

Jim Payne pulled their wagon out of the circle for them. Now they would be the ones to stay behind. Two other wagons, besides the Johnson wagon, had been left behind as the smallpox spread.

Grace wanted to throw herself on Mamma and cry. "No, Grace," said Daddy. "I know you want to help. We can't be sure yet if it's the pox. You mustn't touch her. We're going to have to be brave. " He held her close.

Grace didn't feel brave. She was terrified.

They made a bed for Mamma outside on the ground. "She'll get more air and be more comfortable during the night," said Daddy.

Old Shep stationed himself beside Mamma's bed. Her fever was so high she didn't even know them. She was restless, too. Grace could hear her thrashing in her bed in the night. When she looked out, she could see Old Shep and Daddy by the bed.

Just before dawn, Grace woke with a start. Mamma was coughing. The dreaded flat red spots had appeared in her mouth and on her face and arms. There was no doubt. She had small pox.

As the wagon train got ready to leave, Jim Payne volunteered to stay behind with them. One by one people came to say goodbye. "Hope to see you in California, Mrs. Willis. We're prayin' for you." The simple message of encouragement was said over and over. Mamma was a favorite of almost everyone in the company. She was too weak to reply. But Grace felt sure she knew what they were saying.

Chapter 5

Bill Stokes shook Daddy's hand before the wagon train left them. "She's a good woman, Doc. I hope she makes it. There was another train scheduled to leave Kansas City about a month after us. God willin', Mrs. Willis should be well enough to travel by the time they pass. If we lose any more wagons, we'll have to stop and sit it out until that train catches up. I pray to God the pox stops spreadin'."

As the train left, Grace crawled back under the wagon and cried. *What if Mamma dies?* She hardly dared ask herself the question. When Sid died she thought things couldn't get any worse. This was worse.

The smell of cornbread and salt pork for breakfast brought Grace and Old Shep out from under the wagon. "Everybody needs to know how to cook, Grace," said Jim Payne. He was cooking breakfast.

"That's what Mamma says," said Grace.

"Then how's about if we start a pot of beans for dinner? Reckon you could help me? You've got to boil 'em up first, then let 'em sit for awhile. That gives 'em a jump start if you don't get to soak 'em overnight."

"Sometimes we let them soak all day and start them cooking when we stop for the night," said Grace. She knew how to cook dried beans. She helped Mamma cook. She did all she could to help Mr. Payne, keeping the fire going under the beans. She kept a pot of hot water going for Daddy in case he needed it, too.

Mr. Payne showed her how to make campfire coffee. "You and I will keep a pot goin'. Your Daddy's goin' to need it. He was up all night and he's already wore out from helpin' everybody else."

Daddy and Mr. Payne made a tent to shelter Mamma from the sun. Daddy said Grace couldn't hug her, but she could blow kisses to her. Sometimes Mamma woke up and smiled. Most of the time she slept.

Grace cooked corncakes for their noon meal and some dried apples. Mr. Payne said the corn cakes were as good as any he'd ever eaten. Grace beamed. "They aren't quite so good as Mamma's, but a whole lot better than. . ." She was going to say than Mrs. Swathmore's, when Daddy caught her eye. He didn't approve of children criticizing their elders. Mr. Payne grinned. Grace had a feeling he knew what she hadn't said.

After they'd cleaned up, Mr. Payne said he was going to do some scouting. "Would you like to go along and learn how to be a scout?" he asked. "We can let those beans rest awhile."

Grace was reluctant to leave Mamma.

"Thanks, Jim," Daddy didn't give her a chance to answer for herself. "Don't forget your bonnet, Grace."

"Will Mamma die?" Terrified that he wanted her out of the way when Mama died, she blurted it out before she could stop herself.

Daddy came over and put his arms around her. "She is holding steady, Grace. Right now there is nothing we can do for her. She's asleep. Sleep is exactly what she needs. So it is okay for you to be away for a while. Get your bonnet. She'll be here when you get back. I promise. See, Old Shep is going with you. He knows she can spare him for awhile."

Fighting tears, Grace reluctantly got her bonnet. She wished she could be sure that Daddy wasn't just protecting her from the awful truth.

Chapter 6

THE WAYS OF A SCOUT

It would have been about the most wonderful afternoon ever if Grace hadn't been so worried about Mamma. Mr. Payne showed her how a real scout follows tracks. There were plenty of foot-prints to practice on along the wagon trail. At first they looked for different sizes of footprints. Then she had to guess if they belonged to a man or woman. She tried to pick out a set of prints and follow them. It wasn't as easy as it sounded.

He showed her how to look for disturbances in the environment along the trail. "Look here, Grace. Somebody has been pickin' wildflowers. Can you see where the flowers have been snapped off the stems?"

Now that he pointed it out, she could. There were so many things she hadn't ever noticed before.

After while, he stopped and asked, "Now what does this tell you, Grace?"

Grace looked and looked without seeing anything but footprint upon footprint in the loose dirt by the wagon ruts. She couldn't even find the prints she was supposed to be following. "Look at the direction of this footprint. Somebody ran off into the grass. Somebody about your age, judgin' from the size of the footprints." He showed her the position of the footprint and the bent grass off the trail. "No, there were two of them. One was chasin' the other. See? I'd guess a boy and a girl." He pointed to how the grass was bent. "One person wouldn't leave this pattern. Besides, one set of prints is bigger than the other. Notice that the larger prints are made with a boy's boot." They followed as the bent grass made a loop and joined the trail again. "It was the Swathmore twins. Do you know how I know?" he asked.

"They're always running off!" exclaimed Grace.

Mr. Payne laughed. "You've got a point. You can predict a lot if you know who you're followin'. But look here," He pointed to a tiny shred of fabric caught on the grass, "this is from Ruby Swathmore's dress. I'd say Junior pulled her sash loose. See how this grass has been lashed? He was probably swingin' it around and tauntin' her."

"He's done that before," said Grace. "Mamma mended it for her. But how do you know it's Ruby's?"

"A good scout is always at work noticin' things, even when he isn't scoutin'," said Mr. Payne. "I wonder if you notice how I've kept Old Shep followin' behind? He's a smart dog and a good scout. Why do you reckon I haven't let him run ahead and help us?"

Grace thought for a minute. "He'd cover some of the tracks?"

"Yes, but there's another reason. A dog is a natural tracker. If he has a nose he can follow a scent. But if you're goin' to learn how to track without a dog's nose to help you, Old Shep has to take a back seat."

Grace gave Old Shep a pat. He looked as if he understood Mr. Payne perfectly and was an eager accomplice.

"Now, if I wanted to go through the grass without anybody knowin' I'd been there, what do you suppose I'd have to do?" he asked.

Grace was stumped. "Walk on tip-toe?" It was a guess.

Mr. Payne laughed. "You're close. Sometimes you can't avoid leavin' a trail. But I could take off my boots and go barefoot. Or I could tie some cloth over my feet. Either way I'd leave less of a mark than with these big old boots on. A good tracker could follow me anyway. Still, I could make it harder and slow him down. That would be important if I was on the run."

Where the grass was tall, he showed her how to part it with a stick and step inside, returning the grass to its position behind them with each step. "I wouldn't go in a straight line, either. That way, anybody followin' me would have to stop and study things. That's important when every minute counts. It slows 'em down."

"But what if we're doing the tracking?" asked Grace.

"Well, if you're trackin' somebody, you have to figure they might do the same thing. So you have to have sharp eyes and scan everything around you. Another thing," Mr. Payne continued. "A good scout always watches where he is goin' so he won't get lost. If we couldn't see the wagon from here, what could we look for to guide us back?"

Grace was stumped again. The gray-green, wind-swept prairie grass all looked the same to her. Mr. Payne had her stand and look around. They stood for what seemed a very long time. Then he pointed out how there were small differences in the land formation, an outcropping of rock here, a patch of scrub oak there, a small grove of trees at the base of a hill. "You don't really start to see those things until you look for awhile. The more you look at it, the more the landscape opens up to you. You see things you didn't even know was there. You notice 'em after that because you know every part of this prairie is different."

"You can't tell because you aren't noticing it," concluded Grace.

Mr. Payne didn't answer, but his beaming smile said enough. After awhile, he said, "I think you are worryin' about your mamma."

"I am," she confessed.

"How do you think I know?" he asked.

"You know Mamma's sick?"

"Yes, but there is somethin' I see. What do you reckon it is?" he turned the question back.

Grace considered. "I keep looking at the wagon?"

"Sure enough!" he said, smiling down at her. "Every now and again you look back. We're not bein' followed and your mamma is sick. Lookin' back at the wagon tells me you're concerned about what's goin' on there while you're away. Why don't you pick some wildflowers for your mamma? Then see if you can get back to the wagon without leavin' a trail. I'll come along directly and see if I can follow your tracks. If you can spare him, I'll keep Old Shep with me."

Grace was in a hurry to get back to Mamma. But she tried her best to step carefully, practicing some of the tricks she'd learned. Mamma was asleep when she got to camp, so she saved the wild flowers for later.

When Mr. Payne and Old Shep returned, they had two rabbits. Mr. Payne had them dressed and

41

ready to cook for dinner. "I got these with my slingshot, Grace," he said. "If I was followin' outlaws, or if I was runnin' from them, for that matter, I wouldn't want to make any unnecessary sounds. So I'd use my sling."

"Could you make me a slingshot?" asked Grace.

"I could, but I wouldn't want you tryin' to kill an animal. You have to be an expert shot. It's a sorry thing that we have to kill livin' things to eat. But at least we can be merciful."

"Could you track me back to the wagon?" Grace asked hopefully.

"You did a right good job, Grace," Mr. Payne said. "Especially when you went through the tall grass. But I did find this." He held up a wilted flower. "It fell out of your posy and marked your trail."

Grace's face fell. She'd been so careful.

Mr. Payne patted her on the back. "Don't worry. It takes practice. You're off to a good start. Aren't many folk who could do as well on their first outin'."

"But there are flowers everywhere," protested Grace.

"Ah, yes. But this flower was not where it was supposed to be," said Mr. Payne. "That makes all the difference."

He set a Y-shaped pole right in front of the fire, one on either side. "You can help, Grace. I found this straight branch long enough to reach across. We're goin' to take the bark off." As Grace helped him strip off the bark, he explained, "It needs to be green so it won't burn and there has to be enough branch stickin' out on one side so as we can turn the meat while it cooks."

"If we were following somebody, wouldn't the fire give us away?" asked Grace.

"Good thinkin', Grace. You're right. The smoke would give us away even before the fire."

"So it wouldn't do any good to kill the rabbits," said Grace.

"Well, if I was gettin' real hungry and didn't have anything else to eat, I might have to make a pit fire," said Mr. Payne. He peeled the last of the bark off of the branch. "Now lets get this meat on to roast."

"What's a pit fire?" asked Grace.

"If you can find the right place, it is a good way to hide a fire. You'd dig a pit about a foot across at the top and down about a foot. You get a better fire if you dig down about four or five inches, then scoop out a jug shape until you get down to about twelve inches or so. Then you see which way the wind is blowin'. You want it to blow toward your pit. About a foot away from your pit, in the direction the wind's comin' from, you dig a hole about six inches across and head toward your bigger pit at a slant. The idea is to connect up to your jug so you have an air tunnel that will keep your fire goin'. A fire has to breathe."

Mr. Payne had the rabbits trussed onto the green branch. Setting the branch over the two Y-shaped sticks, he said, "We can leave this cookin' for awhile. Maybe we should look about and see if we can find us some greens for dinner, too." Together they walked out along the trail.

"Old Shep isn't coming," said Grace.

"It looks like he wants to stay with your mamma for awhile," said Mr. Payne. "She's doin' real good, but I think he's tryin' to give your daddy a break. He's a fine dog."

"Do you think he is magic?" asked Grace, wishing immediately that she hadn't asked. It didn't seem like the kind of question you asked a grown-up.

"Well, I don't know much about magic," Mr. Payne said thoughtfully. "But I'll tell you what, Old Shep is the smartest dog I ever met. There is somethin' about him." He hesitated for a moment. "Wise. That's what it is. Old Shep is wise."

That was one of the nice things about Mr. Payne. He didn't make her feel dumb for asking.

Chapter 7

NOT TO BE TRUSTED

Mr. Payne pointed to a plant that had slender, almost diamond-shaped leaves and a long stem covered with tiny, bristly little green seed heads. "This is pigweed. The leaves are very tasty raw and you can eat the seeds when they come on in the summer. You don't find pigweed much except along creek beds or in old buffalo wallows. It likes it here along the trail ruts."

"What's a buffalo wallow?" asked Grace.

"See, water collects in low places after the rain. Buffalo come along and roll in the mud and dust. They worry the soil until plants like pigweed have a good place to grow. Now some of these other plants have to be cooked to taste like anything, like this lambs quarter."

"I know about lambs quarter," said Grace. "Mamma and I put it in our bean soup."

"Yep," he said, "Let's get some of this wild onion, too." He gave Grace his jackknife. "You'll need to dig around the onion bulb. The ground is too dry to pull it up."

"If Old Shep was magic, maybe he could make Mamma well," said Grace as she dug around the wild onions.

"Well, I don't know about that," said Mr. Payne. "Maybe it's like with angels. They're here to help us, but they don't interfere too much with the way things are."

"Then what's the use of it?" asked Grace, pulling the onions free and handing him the jackknife.

"Well, you've got me there," said Mr. Payne. "Sometimes awful bad things happen and there's no gettin' around it. But I'd hate to think of a world without angels, wouldn't you? Maybe it's like that with Old Shep. Maybe he's here to help us get through it—good times and bad times."

He stooped over and pulled the tall grass away from the green stalk of a yucca plant working its way through the grass. "These are real good to eat when they're young and tender like this."

He showed her how to pick the seed pods off a mesquite bush. Opening a pod with his jack-knife, he said, "This pithy part is good to eat. You could eat the seeds if you could crack them, but they're too hard unless you have the right tools."

Grace tasted the pith. It had a brown-sugary taste.

"Mother nature can take good care of you, if you know what to look for," Mr. Payne grinned. "It's all part of bein' a good scout."

Grace was in awe. She'd always thought that being a scout just meant looking for tracks.

The first thing she did when they got back to camp was go over to see Mamma, who was sleeping peacefully. Then she gave Old Shep a big hug. "Thank you," she whispered.

Mr. Payne added their collection of greens to the bean soup. "Is this a good place for a fire pit?" Grace asked.

"Nah, it's a bit windy. Soil is too sandy. It would cave in. Now over there, down by that grove—that's the kind of place you'd probably want to shelter for the night if you were scoutin'. You sure wouldn't want to be sittin' up here on top of a hill for all the world to see. Course we're up here because we want the world to see—anybody comin' will know that there is pox in this wagon and they'd better steer clear or be careful." Nodding back at the grove, he added, "The soil is probably good down there. You wouldn't want to dig too close to tree roots. But the trees and brush would keep the little bit of smoke from your fire pit from bein' seen. The smoke would kind of filter out among the leaves. You'd have to use dry twigs to make your fire, though. Green or wet wood makes a lot of smoke. Even a fire pit can't hide that.

"With a pit you don't need more than a few twigs. That's a good thing. If you're on the run you don't want to be thrashin' around lookin' for firewood."

"How do you know so much about scouting?" Grace asked.

"Well, before I married the Mrs., I was a scout for the army. I traveled all over this country, sometimes by myself. Sometimes I was after somebody and sometimes they was after me! Now we're goin' to settle in California. It is a beautiful country—a great place for a family. It hasn't been a state that long and it's a free state."

Once they'd added their collection of greens to the bean soup, Mr. Payne set her to turning the meat. Grace could hear him quietly talking with Daddy. "I climbed that high ridge back over there. Didn't see any sign of anything comin' from back east—not even a mule train."

"All the wagons we've left behind are well marked with pox signs and off the trail," said Daddy. "God forbid, but if folk haven't survived, the next company will know to set fire to the wagons."

"No sign of Kiowa or Comanche or anybody else," said Mr. Payne. "But there is a wagon pulled over further on up the Trail. Looks like the Swathmore wagon to me, has the same makeshift bonnet. I don't see how it will last the trip. Could be the baby or one of the kids is showin' symptoms. It's too far to go up there now. I'll ride over in the mornin'."

"Be careful," said Daddy. "Hiram Swathmore is a wild card. He's not to be trusted."

"I know what you mean," said Mr. Payne. "But if they need help, I wouldn't want to refuse it."

"If they need a doctor, I can go over when you get back, that is, if Amanda is stable," said Daddy. "She's taking broth. That's a good sign. I sure appreciate you keeping Grace busy this afternoon. There's little she can do here. It was a relief to me to know she was having a good time."

"That little girl of yours is a quick study," said Mr. Payne. "A few more afternoons and I'd make a first rate scout out of her. Shoot, what I didn't teach her she'll learn for herself if she has the opportunity. All she needs is practice."

Grace beamed at the praise.

"Thanks, Jim," said Daddy.

"I'll tell you what," Mr. Payne added. "You got yourself a little philosopher there. She can ask questions that have me stumped."

"That she can," said Daddy, smiling.

Later, as they dished up supper, Mr. Payne said, "I forgot an important thing, Grace. If you dig a fire pit, it's a good idea to take the sod off the top of the big hole. Save it. When you're ready to put out the fire, you can fill the hole with the dirt you took out. If you were tryin' to cover your tracks, you want to leave things lookin' like they did when you got there. If you set the sod back over the top it'd be pretty hard to tell anybody was there. Anyway, it is a good idea to try to leave things the way Mother Nature has them. That's why Mr. Stokes is such a stickler for leavin' our campsites clean when the train moves on."

They had a tasty dinner. The best part was that Daddy got Mamma to eat some soup. She was even alert enough to blow a kiss to Grace.

Later, Grace tried digging a fire pit by the wagon. Mr. Payne was right. It was too sandy. She got her jug shaped hole scooped out, but it collapsed before she could start the air tunnel.

When it was dark, Daddy tucked her into bed in the wagon. "I love you Grace. And Mamma loves you, too, more than you can know. Don't ever forget that, no matter what happens. I'm proud of you. Don't ever forget that, either." Then he gave her a kiss on the forehead. "You can sleep at ease tonight. I have every reason to believe Mamma's coming around."

As soon as Daddy was out of sight, Grace remembered something she had tucked away in the box that held her dresses, the ones she was to have when they got to California. The handkerchief Grandma Rhoads gave her had been there since the morning they left St. Louis. Removing it from the box, she tucked it in the sleeve of her nightgown and quietly slipped back under the covers. Tomorrow she would give it to Mamma to remind her of how much she was loved.

Grace fell into a deep, untroubled sleep. She wasn't sure what happened after that, but when she awoke early the next morning, the wagon was moving. Mr. and Mrs. Swathmore were sitting where Daddy and Mamma should have been. Their children were fast asleep on the featherbed Mamma kept tied up to the bent wood bows that supported the canvas top. They didn't use it on the trail. Mamma was saving it for their new home in California.

"Girl," said Mr. Swathmore, "your Mamma and Pappa died in the night from the pox." Grace sat still, too stunned to speak or to cry. Mamma said that Daddy wouldn't get smallpox. And Daddy said Mamma was getting better. Something was terribly wrong. Grace didn't trust the Swathmores any more than her Daddy did. But trapped in the wagon, there was nothing she could do.

Chapter 8

NOTHING TO CALL HER OWN

"Your Mamma was good to me, Girl. With her last breath, she asked me to take care of you. It's the least we can do for her," said Mrs. Swathmore. "Here. You hold the baby."

She could hear the Swathmores talking. "We got us a good start. We'll make for that Cherokee Outlet and follow the Cimarron River. Best put some miles between us and the Trail," Mr. Swathmore said. "I reckon we'll hit the Cimarron if we head due south. The Canadian cuts through somewheres below the Cimarron."

Mrs. Swathmore had a whole string of complaints and reasons why they couldn't do it. "Like as not we'll be killed by Injuns."

"Shut your infernal yappin' mouth, Woman! A chance like this don't come every day. They ain't havin' Injun trouble in Oklahoma Territory. If you want to sit behind and die of the pox you can stay. But I'm a goin'."

Grace looked out the back to see the two Swathmore oxen. The Willis milk-cow and horses—both laden with packs—were tied behind, too. Old Shep was nowhere in sight. Her heart sank. Nothing in the landscape looked familiar.

Some things were missing from the wagon: a box of medical books Daddy had for the medical school and medical supplies donated for a hospital. In their place were things from the Swathmore wagon. No more was said about what happened. She didn't dare ask. She was terrified of Mr. Swathmore—she'd seen what he could do with that belt of his when he was angry. She wanted to scream and cry. But no tears would come. She felt hollow inside as if there was nothing left.

She wondered if she could run away and get back to Mamma and Daddy. It was as if Mr. Swathmore could read her mind. "Don't get any smart ideas about tryin' to go back to the Santa Fe, Girl. Your Ma and Pa is dead and buried. You'd never get back to the Trail alive. This country is full of wild animals. You can't see 'em, but they can see you. They'd track down a little girl like you and have her for supper. You wouldn't last the night." He patted the gun that lay across his lap. "I'd shoot you before I'd let that happen to you, Girl."

They traveled for days without seeing another living creature. Being cooped up with the Swathmore twins in the wagon was torture. They pulled her hair, jabbed her with their elbows, and pinched. It was no good telling on them. Mrs. Swathmore always blamed her. It seemed like one never ending fight with crying from the children, screaming from Mrs. Swathmore, and Mr. Swathmore threatening to take off his belt and give all of them a good thrashing, including Mrs. Swathmore.

At night, Grace tossed and turned under the wagon. She tried thinking about home and St. Louis, but she couldn't stay focused. She was gnawed by worry about Mamma and Daddy. *Daddy said Mamma was getting better. Why don't they come for me?* She refused to believe that they were dead.

She clung to the handkerchief Grandma Rhoads gave her, trying to remember that she was loved. She kept it tucked inside her dress where nobody could see it.

After they were several days out from the Trail, Mr. Swathmore let them walk. The twins were usually too lazy. Grace was grateful for any excuse to be out of the wagon. She tried to inconspicuously practice walking along without leaving a trail and watching for land formations to keep her mind off of things. She hardly dared hope, but at the back of her mind she wondered if she could ever break free and escape. If she did, she had to be prepared. But she was always under Mr. Swathmore's watchful eye. Sometimes when he looked at her, he patted his gun. It was his way of reminding her that she was going nowhere except with them.

They followed buffalo trails through the rough plains and passed what she felt sure was a buffalo wallow. Where there were no trails, they stayed close to the wide, shallow, treeless banks of the Cimarron River as it wound through the prairie like a ribbon thrown on the floor. In the evening, Grace built the campfire, milked the cow, and helped Mrs. Swathmore with the cooking. They lived on fried cornbread and salt pork taken from the Willis food supply.

One evening, Grace picked some wild greens. "What do you think you're doin'?" demanded Mrs. Swathmore. "I won't have my family eatin' weeds." Grabbing the wild greens, she threw them away.

They slept in their clothes and nobody washed up, not even Grace, unless they were camped by the river. Mr. Swathmore said it was a waste of water.

The twins ran wild when they made camp. Otis and Myrtle clung to Grace. When she wasn't doing chores, she played games with the two of them or told them stories. Even Ruby and Junior stopped to listen when she told a story.

The country ahead began to look even rougher and wilder than before. Red sandstone rock mounds and white gypsum broke through the gray-green prairie grass. One evening just as they stopped to make camp for the night, Junior yelled. "Get the gun, Pa. There's a varmint comin' after us." He pointed back along the path they'd been following.

Mr. Swathmore had his gun in a flash. He put the gun down almost as suddenly as he grabbed it. "That ain't no varmit. Looks like your Pa's dog, Girl. Done followed the wagon."

Grace's heart leapt with joy. Old Shep came bounding along the wagon tracks. *He's come to help me! Maybe Daddy is coming, too.*

"Best be good and sure they ain't nobody followin' him." Mr. Swathmore seemed to be thinking the same thing. Grace thought he seemed afraid. "Get back in the wagon, all of you," he ordered. While they waited in the wagon, Mr. Swathmore climbed up a gypsum rock mound and looked around. He was there for what seemed like a long time, gun in hand, watching.

Old Shep lay down beside the wagon. Grace was on pins and needles, fearful that if her father followed Old Shep, Mr. Swathmore might see him and shoot him. She longed to jump down from the wagon and throw her arms around Old Shep for comfort. But she didn't dare. If Mr. Swathmore said to do something, they'd better do it. Even Mrs. Swathmore obeyed.

Old Shep looked up at her. Somehow she knew from his look that her Daddy wasn't following.

Finally Mr. Swathmore returned. "Ain't nobody comin' after us." Looking at Old Shep, he said, "Smart dog to follow all that way. Reckon I could use a good tracker."

After that, Grace wasn't so lonely. Old Shep seemed to know when she was the most fright-ened and homesick. He snuggled up next to her under the wagon at night, putting his cold nose against her cheek. When it was day, he followed along by the wagon, keeping his distance from her. Grace knew better than to say anything about Old Shep. It would have been an excuse for Ruby and Junior to torment him. She remem-bered what Daddy said, "I'm not so sure you can say that Old Shep *belongs* to anyone."

One morning Mr. Swathmore left them camped by the river. He took Old Shep and one of the horses to look for a safe place to ford. It was nearly noon when they returned. "Found a place where it's wide and shallow," Mr. Swath-more reported. "River's still runnin' low. Won't be long before spring rains set in if I ain't mis-taken. A body'd have to whip his weight in wild cats to cross oncet the rains start."

When they forded the Cimarron, Grace was grateful for the big wagon bed. The waters were red like the red dirt on the banks. They couldn't see the bottom. Mr. Swathmore crossed on horseback, leading the animals that had been tied behind the wagon. Their hoofs stirred up a nasty smell from the sand and stagnant pools of water. It was deeper close to the middle, spreading out to the far bank. There the Cimarron flowed rapidly. Fortunately, the animals didn't have to swim more than a few feet to get across. Once the animals were across, Mr. Swathmore rode back and led the Willis team of six oxen, pulling the wagon. Their hooves and wagon wheels stirred up more of the brackish, moldy smell. Near the middle of the river, the oxen began to swim. Old Shep followed behind, swimming just past the wake left by the wagon.

Buoyed by the flowing river, the wagon wheels left the bottom. Mrs. Swathmore started screaming in short bursts, "Oh! Oh! Oh no! We're sinking. Oh no! I didn't come all this way to drown!"

The twins were delighted. They tried to rock the wagon and held the baby out over the water, "Baby's goin' a drop! Baby's goin' a drown."

Grace felt pretty sure they wouldn't actually drop the baby. They just wanted to scare everyone. It worked.

Mrs. Swathmore went into hysterics. Grace could no longer understand what she was yelling. It was one long terrified scream. Otis and Myrtle cried, holding on to Grace.

The big wagon was designed to ford more difficult spots than this one, even with all the chaos coming from inside. They were soon across without taking on water or losing anything or anyone from the wagon.

The twins got a belting for threatening the baby and all the goods in the wagon. They said it was Grace's idea, but for once, they had to take the punishment. Grace couldn't help feeling sorry for them, though. When Mr. Swathmore used his belt, it was a terrible thing.

Once across, the land along the West bank of the River was cut through with a wide, creek that wound its way around pockets of rich land. They continued on for another three days following the creek before Mr. Swathmore decided to settle. "This here would be a fine piece of land to own," he said. "One of these days they'll be opening up this territory. We'll be here. Finders keepers."

It was a lovely site, set in a crook of land where the creek was joined by a little stream fed by a fresh spring. The loveliness was lost on Mrs. Swathmore, who began complaining about how desolate it was the minute she got out of the wagon.

"We'll winter here; give me a place to do some trappin'. The North Canadian River can't be more than a few days south. I'd rather get my bearin's on the river and come back for our things than get too far south and have a bunch of Mexicans tryin' to steal us blind."

Mrs. Swathmore was more than glad to stop, even though she complained. They lived in the big wagon, cooking over a campfire until Mr. Swathmore finished carving a dugout into the side of a hill. He felled trees for logs to finish out the front of the dugout. They unloaded the big wagon, furnishing the dugout with things that belonged to Grace's family. "It's rightful payment for taking in an orphan," Mrs. Swathmore said.

Not a day passed that Mrs. Swathmore didn't remind Grace of how grateful she should be. To Grace it felt like Mrs. Swathmore was the one who should be grateful. Grace milked the cow twice a day and carried water from the spring every morning to fill the kettle that hung over the open fire outside the dugout. She carried more water to fill the large speckled blue enamel bucket that held drinking water. It was Grace who washed and dried the dishes after meals, swept the dugout, cared for the baby, and minded the younger children.

The twins tormented her. When Junior tore her dress, Mrs. Swathmore said, "What'd you expect? Boys will be boys. You shouldn't a got in his way." When Ruby took her doll, Mrs. Swathmore said, "It ain't fair for an orphan to have more than my own rightful daughter." When they broke her tea set, Mrs. Swathmore said, "It'll teach you a lesson." They were the only toys she had been allowed to bring with her when she left her home in St. Louis.

Sometimes it felt like there was nothing left she could call her own. In moments like that, she wished with all her heart that they had never left St. Louis. But she wasn't allowed to cry. Any hint of tears set Mrs. Swathmore to wailing over what a trial it was to be responsible for an orphan or Mr. Swathmore threatening to take off his belt and give her something to cry about. Except she did cry, inside, in the deep places nobody could see or hear. They couldn't keep her from doing that. In the night when she felt afraid and alone, she cried without tears. Her heart cried for Mamma and Daddy, for Sid, for her family in St. Louis, for her comfortable, safe home, and for everything that seemed lost forever. She clung to the lace edged handkerchief Grandma Rhodes had given her, trying to remember what it was like to be loved.

Sometimes she slipped out of the dugout after everyone was asleep and slept beside Old Shep. He was her only comfort. "I wish you were magic, Old Shep. I wish there were an angel who looked out for me," she whispered to him one night. Then she remembered what Mamma said to her the day of the auction. "You are going to have to decide if you are a part of this and ready to accept an adventure, or if you're going to cling to your misery and lock out the world." *Well, Mamma, this is no adventure, at least not the right sort. But I'm not going to waste my time feeling sorry for myself any more. If you and Daddy can't find me, then I will find you.*

Chapter 9

APPLE DUMPLINGS

Mrs. Swathmore said she had a nervous condition that required her to spend most of her time in the featherbed. The only thing she did for the family was to throw together meals. "I can't see why a great big girl like Grace can't be doing the cooking when I'm so ill," she complained.

Mr. Swathmore wouldn't allow it. "You learned on me Mrs. I've eaten enough burned beans for a lifetime. I ain't goina' be learned on again. Haul your lazy carcass out of that bed and get a man some food he can eat."

Grace wasn't allowed to eat with the family. She had to wait until the others had their fill. "Don't get any uppity ideas about bein' part of the family just because we took you in," Mrs. Swathmore said. When it was her turn to eat,

Grace was lucky to have enough cornbread and beans to feel full. There was usually some milk left, but the meat was almost always gone. Grace was just as glad. She could hardly bear to think about eating some poor animal that died in a trap.

The hardest job was watching the children. Grace tried to involve them in helping by making it fun, the way her mother had done. The little ones tried to please. But the twins constantly interfered. They learned quickly that Grace could be blamed for just about anything that went wrong. When that happened, Mr. Swathmore took off his belt and gave Grace three or four smacks across the legs for punishment. Ruby and Junior stood behind him and made faces at her.

They got their share of strappings, too. Grace dreaded it, though, because they always blamed her and took it out on her when Mr. Swathmore wasn't around. Sometimes her arms were black and blue from being pinched, scratched, punched, and kicked.

Bedtime was the only time Grace seemed to have any influence over the twins. All she had to do was promise a story and even Ruby and Junior would get ready for bed. No matter how tired she was, Grace told them a story every night after they were in bed. She told them every story she could remember: stories from the Bible, stories from books she'd had at school, and stories her mother had told her. The story the twins liked best was *Aladdin and His Wonderful*

Lamp. They would try to act it out the next day, but almost always got into a fight over who was Aladdin. "Ain't no call for Junior to be Aladdin just because he's a boy," Ruby complained. Grace agreed with her, but she knew better than to say anything. Both of the twins would turn on her if she tried to have anything to do with their games. Otis and Myrtle had to take whatever parts they were assigned or suffer the consequences—usually a good cuffing.

Mr. Swathmore was busy clearing and breaking the land. Most days he kept Junior and Ruby busy picking up rocks and branches. He was the only one who could get any work out of them. Sometimes, though, he took his gun and disappeared on horseback. He was gone for days at a time. While he was away, Grace did the cooking. Mrs. Swathmore demanded to be served in bed. Ruby and Junior were at their worst then, without Mr. Swathmore to put them to work or to threaten with his belt. The only thing that seemed to get them to stop tormenting her was the promise that she'd tell them the story of Aladdin at bedtime. Sometimes she had to tell two stories because Otis and Myrtle wanted another favorite. It was a small price to pay for peace.

One day Mr. Swathmore returned smelling of corn whiskey. He'd been all the way to the Canadian River to a trading post run by a Spanish trapper and his Pawnee wife. The whiskey did little to improve his short temper. The supply he had on the trail had long since run out. Grace was sorry that he'd found another supply. She'd learned to stay away from him as much as possible when he was drinking. He was likely as not to give anyone a beating who disturbed him, including Mrs. Swathmore. Just about anything sent him into a rage.

Every morning Mr. Swathmore checked his traps and brought back animals he'd caught. Grace couldn't stand to look at the poor things. He carefully skinned them and cured their pelts. The meat was used for cooking or to make jerky. Mr. Swathmore made jerky by hanging thin strips of meat over a rack made from sticks and thin strips of leather. When the wind dried out the meat, he coated the strips with fat to seal them from mold.

One morning he returned from checking his traps empty handed. "Somebody's been tamperin' with the traps," he said, throwing them down. "Now I gotta' fix 'em." They hadn't seen any sign of people since they'd left the wagon train. Mr. Swathmore hadn't found any tracks to give him a clue as to the thief, either. Grace could tell that he was troubled.

"Grace did it!" yelled Junior. Mr. Swathmore told him to shut up before he took off his belt.

Mrs. Swathmore began nagging. "You've got enough pelts to go to the tradin' post. When are we goin'? I'm starved for company. You can't expect me to live out here without seein' anybody day after day. It's not right for a woman to be without company."

"Ain't no company at the tradin' post that's fit company. Just that Pawnee woman. You fancy yourself makin' up to an Injun woman?"

It didn't matter how many times he told her to shut up her infernal yapping, Mrs. Swathmore was soon at it again. It wasn't long before the Swathmores left for the trading post, taking the wagon. Mrs. Swathmore's nervous condition didn't prevent her from making the trip. She wanted to leave the children with Grace, but the twins set up such a howl that Mr. Swathmore told them to shut up and get in the wagon, leaving Grace and Old Shep to look after the place for the five days it would take them to go and return.

For Grace, it seemed like a holiday. There was plenty of work to be done, but there would be free time, too, and no twins to make life miserable.

That night she put beans on to soak. She was just about to fall asleep when it occurred to her that it would be a good time to escape. It wasn't the first time she'd thought of trying to escape. It had been on her mind since that first morning when she woke up to find the Swathmores in the wagon. But caution told her that she wouldn't get far without careful planning. Unexpected early summer rains had swollen the creek until it was running up to its banks. That meant the Cimarron River would be nearly impossible to cross until late summer or early fall. Her best bet would be to make for the Santa Fe Trail when streambeds were low. There'd be enough time to make it to the Trail before fall frosts. There would be other wagon trains headed for California and on their way to Kansas City with supplies to trade. If her parents were still alive she knew that they would be looking for her.

In the morning she started the pot of beans cooking and made a pot of fluffy apple dumplings with dried apples. She intended to enjoy having them all to herself. Mrs. Swathmore didn't know how to make apple dumplings and refused any suggestions.

As she worked, she thought about what she'd need for her escape. Water. That wouldn't be hard until she had to leave the Cimarron. She'd have to have a canteen. Dried beans wouldn't be hard to carry, but they wouldn't be safe to eat if she couldn't cook them. Oats would be better. Mr. Swathmore had oat seed. Some of his jerky would be good, too. She'd have to travel light and forage once she was a safe distance away. Before morning was over, she'd decided on starting a stockpile in her hide out.

The hide out was a dry cave Old Shep found among the rocks along the creek not long after Mr. Swathmore finished the dugout. Both she and Old Shep understood that it had to be kept secret from everyone, especially the twins. She escaped more than one beating by hiding out there when Mr. Swathmore had drunk too much corn whiskey.

She raided Mr. Swathmore's seed supply for oats, tying a couple of big handfuls up in a rag. If she took more, they'd be missed. A few dried apples were tied up in another rag. Setting them aside, she went on about her work, all the while thinking through her escape plan.

It was late afternoon when Old Shep's low growl alerted her. They had company. She was busy taking in a wash she'd hung out to dry early that morning. Two men rode up. From the look of it, they had been riding for a long time. They were unshaven and dirty. Mamma always said you shouldn't judge people by how they look. But something about the way these two looked made Grace uneasy.

Chapter 10

NO TIME FOR TEARS

"You, girl. Get your Pa for me," said the taller of the men, looking down at her from his horse. Scraggly black hair hung down his shoulders. A wispy moustache and untrimmed beard gave him a cruel look.

"Papa isn't here right now," said Grace. "May I get you some water? We have little enough to eat, but there's cornbread and beans." Even though they'd never had visitors, Grace knew that the laws of hospitality in the wilderness were unwavering. Strangers were offered food and refreshment without question.

"Now that would be right accomodatin' of you, Missy," said the second man, tipping his hat. He was broad in the shoulders and had a large stomach. "A pretty thing, ain't she Dillan? And such fine manners. Real quality folk." He laughed an unpleasant laugh that made his belly shake.

"Your Ma here?" he asked.

"No sir. I thought you were my Mamma and Papa when I heard horses," said Grace, making up a story. "They should be back any time if you want to wait. I have supper on but you can eat now if you like." Something told her she'd better not say she was alone and didn't expect to see anybody for another four days.

Old Shep bristled. Grace was uneasy, too. She didn't like the way the man with the big belly leered at her.

The men dismounted and sat under a shade tree while Grace fetched drinking water, corn-bread, and dipped beans out of the iron pot that had been slowly cooking over the fire all day. "Beans and no meat. Not much of a meal for two hard-working men," said the man called Dillan. "Reckon she's holdin' back on us, Leon?"

"They're made with salt pork, Sir," said Grace. "It's what we have for supper. But there are apple dumplings for dessert."

"Your Pa got anything a man would like to drink?" asked Dillan when she brought the dumplings. "Man gets thirsty after ridin' all day."

"I can make you some coffee," she offered.

"Nah, we was thinkin' of somethin' stronger than coffee," said Leon, smirking.

She brought water for the horses while the men ate the apple dumplings. When she returned, Dillan put his plate down. "Reckon I'll have a look around," he said. With that he got up and walked to the dugout. "Come on Leon, let's see what little Miss is holding back on us. I bet there's more in there than coffee."

"You was thinkin' of some private reserve?" Leon laughed in a way that gave Grace the shivers.

Old Shep placed himself between Grace and the dugout. Suddenly she realized that he was trying to protect her. She stayed outside with him. The two men called to each other. "Don't tell me there's nothing to drink in here," said Leon. She could hear tin plates crashing to the floor and a string of curse words. She'd never heard anything like it, even from Mr. Swathmore at his worst.

"Lookie here, Dillan. Now why didn't little Missy offer us some of Pappa's corn whiskey? That was downright inhospitable, holdin' back on us like that." A silence followed. Grace was pretty sure they were helping themselves to the whiskey. She stood rooted to the spot, not knowing what to do.

After awhile, Leon called, "Over here, Dillan. Here's a genuine featherbed. Don't that beat all?"

"This here's a real high class setup!" Dillan called back.

"I have a mind to have me a nap," said Leon. There were peals of laughter from both of the men as they came staggering out of the dugout, dragging the featherbed between them. They were almost too drunk to stand up.

Old Shep had been pacing back and forth toward the creek. Now he jumped up on Grace, nearly knocking her down. He ran toward the creek, turned and came back, jumping on her again. Unfrozen at last, Grace followed him as fast as she could run. Behind her, she could hear the men howling with laughter as they tore up the bed, sending feathers flying.

"Where did that little Missy get off to?" called Leon in an angry voice.

"I think she went that'a way," said Dillan.

She could hear Leon coming after her. She crawled into the secret place, hoping Old Shep wouldn't growl and give them away. She needn't have worried. Old Shep seemed to know exactly what to do. Leon beat the bushes along the creek, cursing as he went.

He was not far from the entrance to the secret place when Dillan yelled, "Quit fussing over that girl, Leon." Grace hardly dared to breathe. "Get them horses. It's gettin' late. Let's get out of here before her Pa gets back with a gun. Ain't no kind of a sot goinna' leave a little girl like that alone all day. No sense in gettin' bullets in your backside when we can get good money out of them horses."

Grace lay in the secret place shaking. She could hear the brush crashing, then the whinny of horses being led by the strangers. Old Shep was warm and comforting. After awhile he left, returning in a few minutes. She knew it was safe then.

The horses were gone, but the oxen and cow were still there. The featherbed was ripped apart. Feathers were all over the ground blowing here and there in the gentle breeze. The dugout floor was a sea of tin plates, dried beans, pots and utensils. The corn whiskey jug was empty. Almost everything on the kitchen shelves had been thrown on the floor. The bean soup and apple dumplings survived because they were by the fire outside.

There wasn't time for tears. Grace began picking up all the feathers she could collect before they blew away, stuffing them back into the featherbed. When she'd gathered as many as she could, she sewed up the slashed places. By then it was dark. She left the featherbed out under the tree to air. Afraid to stay in the dugout in the dark, she took what was left of dinner and crept back to her secret place. She shared with Old Shep, even the apple dumpling. Then she fell into an exhausted sleep next to him.

Chapter 11

ESCAPE

The next two days were spent restoring order. Early on the fifth day she put on a pot of beans and dragged the featherbed back inside, making it up so it would be ready for Mr. and Mrs. Swathmore. It was late afternoon when she heard them coming. The sky was turning shades of pink and purple as the wagon pulled up in front of the dugout. She had bean soup and cornbread waiting.

Overcome with relief, Grace ran out to meet the wagon, breathlessly trying to tell what happened. Mr. Swathmore leapt out of the wagon. He reeked of corn whiskey. His mood was the worse for it, too. "Horses? Stolen? You good for nothin' idiot girl! You let somebody steal us blind?"

There were still feathers in the yard, too scattered for Grace to collect them. "My featherbed!" Mrs. Swathmore screamed. She smelled of corn whiskey, too. Jumping out of the wagon in a rage, she grabbed Grace. Slapping her hard across the face, she hissed, "I have a mind you did this yourself out of sheer spite, you ungrateful orphan."

Mr. Swathmore picked up a fallen branch. He began pulling away the leaves. "Come here, Girl!" he demanded. Mrs. Swathmore pushed Grace toward him.

"Hit her Pa, hit her!" yelled Junior. "Hit her good!" He and Ruby jumped up and down in the wagon crying, "Hit her! Hit her!" as if they were cheering for their home team.

Otis and Myrtle jumped out of the wagon and ran to her, arms outstretched, crying, "Don't hurt Grace, Pa. Please don't hurt Grace."

"Get those infernal brats out of my way!" Mr. Swathmore pulled Otis and Myrtle away from Grace, shoving them toward Mrs. Swathmore. Seizing her by the arm, he lashed Grace's legs with a swift stroke of the branch and struck her hard across the back. Old Shep jumped on him in a snarling fury, biting the arm that held the branch. Dropping it, Mr. Swathmore cursed, dancing with pain. "Get the gun from the wagon, Mrs. I'm shootin' that dog. Don't you even move, Girl. You're goin'a get the beatin' of your life."

Chapter 11

Grace ran, Old Shep behind her. It was already getting dark down by the creek. She ran toward the creek bank, trying to get as far away from Mr. Swathmore as she could. Junior and Ruby ran screaming after her, "Get her Pa! Get the good for nothin' idiot girl."

Behind them, Mr. Swathmore raged, "If I ever set eyes on your ugly face again, Girl, I'll shoot you *and* that good for nothin' dog."

Terrified, Otis and Myrtle tried to run after Grace, too, calling, "Don't go, Grace. We love you, Grace."

Mrs. Swathmore brought the gun, screaming at the children to come back. "And somebody stop that baby from her infernal cryin'," she squawked. The baby, left in the wagon in all the excitement, was shrieking as loud as the rest of them.

Mr. Swathmore was too drunk to follow very far. He yelled at the children to get out of the way before he shot them, too. A few precious bullets were wasted as he shot in the direction Grace and Old Shep ran. At least it got Junior and Ruby off her trail. Grace knew he'd cool off. Mrs. Swathmore wouldn't want to lose her help, either. So he'd come after her, but not tonight.

The night closed in, but Grace kept running. Old Shep ran just ahead of her, leading the way. They reached a place where the creek split, winding its way around a small, sandy island. Grace knew the island. The creek was shallow on the near side. It was so dark out they could hardly see, too dark to go on. Old Shep waded across to the island. Grace followed. They threw themselves down, panting. Grace's legs were caked with blood from the lashing Mr. Swathmore had given her. Her back ached from the hard blow he landed. She had long since outgrown her shoes. Her bare feet were bruised and barked from tripping over roots and rocks in the dark. She soaked her legs and feet in the cold water. "We're never going back, Old Shep. Never. Even if it means we die out here in the woods all alone." Old Shep looked at her knowingly. He always seemed to know exactly what to do. He found a dry spot in the tall grass and began circling around, mashing it down. They slept there on the bed he created, curled up together.

Her only regret was leaving Otis and Myrtle. They were two little lights in a dark, dark place.

Chapter 12

SOME WOULD CALL IT MAGIC

The sky above hinted at the first light before dawn when Grace sat up. She'd been dreaming. In her dream, she saw an angel. He didn't have wings, but he must have been an angel. He was dressed in silver-white with starlight shining from him. His hair and short beard were silver, too. The angel knelt beside her, bending over he drew a heart on her forehead with the index finger of his left hand. "Rest, child," he said. It seemed so real she almost expected to see him kneeling there when she awoke. But her only company was Old Shep, sitting up beside her. A gentle wind bent the grass and rippled the water in the creek. The pink and gold of dawn were spreading across the sky.

Mr. Swathmore set traps all up and down the creek. Grace knew that they'd have to put miles between them before they'd be safe. How they would live, she did not know. But she couldn't go back. Mr. Swathmore would wake up with a splitting headache, feeling too sick to get an early start, but he'd be after them all too soon. And unlike Grace, he knew the woods far up and down the river. He knew how to track, too. So she and Shep were going to have to be careful from now on because they couldn't outrun him if he caught up.

She took a deep drink of water. "We'll have to stay along the creek as long as we can," she told Old Shep. Grace had learned a thing or two about living in the wild because she hadn't forgotten what Mr. Payne taught her. She'd kept her eyes and ears open when they left the Santa Fe Trail, too. She'd even learned from Mr. Swathmore. He was an unlikely teacher, but he knew the wild. Grace secretly watched when she could. So she knew that he'd have no trouble following them up to the island. "We're going to leave tracks going south, Old Shep. He'll expect us to head in that direction. Then we'll double back and hide out on the other side of the creek past the dugout where he'll least expect to find us. We'll try to find our way back to the Santa Fe Trail. That's all I know to do." Old Shep wagged his tail as if he understood and agreed to the plan. It was uncanny the way he seemed to know exactly what needed to be done. "Maybe you are magic, Old Shep. We're going to need all the magic we can get. Magic and good straight thinking."

Chapter 12

She walked back across the creek, leaving clear footprints on the sandy bank, heading south until the creek meandered to the right, leaving a wide, meadow. "He'll think we're going to follow the wagon tracks down toward the trading post. So we'd better leave some tracks for him, Old Shep." Picking up a short, stout stick, she headed across the meadow, disturbing the tall grass as she went. She wanted Mr. Swathmore to think she didn't know anything about hiding her tracks. Old Shep did his part, too, capering through the grass and mashing it down so their passage couldn't be missed.

When they found the trail made by the wagon and oxen going to and from the trading post, Grace followed it until the sun was up. "We are making it too easy for Mr. Swathmore," she said to Old Shep. She threw the stick as far up the trail as she could send it. He ran after it, bringing it back and leaving a confusion of tracks. When she caught up, he ran out toward an outcropping of rocks that stood far in the distance, opposite the creek and off the trail, leaving trampled grass behind him. Grace got the idea. She ran in that direction, leaving grass askew, stepping in his tracks. She carefully turned back well before she reached the rocks. Hopefully Mr. Swathmore would follow Old Shep's trail before he figured out that her tracks weren't there.

Weaving her way carefully, she reached the trail further on ahead. Once on the trail again, she left footprints now and then where the wagon had made ruts, then began to be more careful, walking on the grass between, only occasionally leaving a footprint. She tried to remember everything Mr. Payne had taught her. *Slow him down. Make him work.* Old Shep seemed to have the same idea. He ran back and forth over the path she took to the rocks, making it harder to tell where her footprints left off, then looped his way back to the wagon trail. Once there, he ran way ahead, disappearing from view. Returning to Grace, he trotted carefully through the tall grass far to the side of the trail, leaving little evidence of his passing.

Ahead, the creek wound its way closer to the trail. Between the creek and trail was a stand of tall grass leading to another outcropping of rocks, this one bordering the creek. Old Shep made for these rocks.

Grace left the trail, heading toward the creek to meet him. She carefully parted the tall grass, stepping into it and replacing it as she went, the way Mr. Payne taught her. Mr. Swathmore might find it later, but he'd likely go toward the outcropping of rocks, then back down the trail, especially with Old Shep's tracks leading so far ahead. When she reached the rocks, Grace scrambled as fast as she could. Old Shep was waiting for her next to a large pool made by the creek.

It was the perfect place to cross without leaving signs, too. Large rocks made a good stepping off place into the water. On the other side minnows chased each other in the shallow water of a long sandy stretch of creek bed. The water flowed fast enough to erase any evidence of tracks. Grace and Old Shep followed the shallow water until they reached a rocky bank where they climbed out to the other side of the creek, leaving little, if any evidence that they'd been there.

Up ahead was the island where they'd spent the night. It was well into the morning. Mr. Swathmore could appear any minute. Grace was also worried about traps, fearing that Old Shep might get caught if they stayed close to the creek. They'd been lucky the night before. She had been in such a rush to get away, she hadn't thought about traps. *Maybe it wasn't luck. Maybe Old Shep knows what he is doing.* She used to wonder if Old Shep could be magic. There hadn't been much magic in her life since Sid Johnson died. Everything had gone from bad to worse. She thought of the angel in the dream that seemed so real. Some would call that magic.

It was a bright sunny day. She could feel the warmth of the sun filtering through the trees as they climbed out on the rocks. They made a wide berth of the creek moving upstream, taking to the less covered area above the creek bed in order to avoid traps. She stopped periodically, listening for Mr. Swathmore, cautioning Old Shep to stay with her. It wasn't necessary. They were working like a well-practiced team.

It was almost noon when she heard Junior shouting. "Up here, Pa. That good-for-nothing girl went this way." She needn't have bothered to stop and listen for Mr. Swathmore. Junior made enough racket to alert anyone within shouting distance. Asking Old Shep to stay put, Grace stole back through the brush where she could see Mr. Swathmore and Junior headed downstream along the banks following her tracks.

"Get back here, Junior. This here creek is seeded with traps. Don't go steppin' in one. I reckon that girl may have got herself caught. Serve her right. Dog's too smart to get trapped."

Junior reluctantly fell back. "What's she doin' here?" he cried, looking back. Ruby came up just on his heels. "She's been followin' us, Pa. Make her go back. Trackin' is men's work."

"I'm better at trackin' than Junior and he knows it," said Ruby.

"Shut up and stay back of me, both of you," said Mr. Swathmore. "First rule of trackin' is to keep yer mouth shut and yer eyes open. You two will let the whole danged wilderness know you're comin' if you don't shut your infernal yappers."

Soon they'd be at the island and set out on the trail she'd left for them. She'd have to put as much distance between them as possible before they turned back. Mr. Swathmore was no fool. He wouldn't follow long before he'd figure that she had crossed back. If they were lucky, he'd search along the creek for awhile. But she couldn't count on it. As careful as she and Old Shep were, it wouldn't be too difficult for him to follow if he crossed to the opposite bank. Speed was more important than anything now. Speed and distance. Mr. Payne said that sometimes you just have to run for it.

Chapter 13

MAKING A RUN FOR IT

They walked rapidly in the grassland that bordered the creek. She wanted to run, but she knew she had to conserve her energy. It would be a long day.

As they neared the homestead, Grace decided to slip back and collect some supplies. Mrs. Swathmore was likely to be in bed. She'd have to avoid Otis and Myrtle. If they saw her and Mr. Swathmore found out, he'd beat them. But if she were to make it to the Santa Fe Trail, she needed water and at least the oats and dried apple she had set aside.

Leaving Old Shep to watch on the opposite bank, Grace waded across where the creek was at its shallowest, mentally rehearsing every move she would make. The bank was rock covered, so she needn't worry about leaving tracks.

The oats and dried apples she'd meant to put in her hideout were probably still sitting where she'd left them in her haste to clean up. That would make it easy enough if she could get into the dugout unobserved. Her father's hunting knife, flint and steel pouch, and tin canteen were hanging alongside Mr. Swathmore's trapping gear in a lean-to he'd built to store prairie grass for the animals. If it came to that, she'd forgo going into the dugout. But the canteen, flint and steel pouch, and knife were essential.

Myrtle and Otis were too busy playing on the wagon, parked where it had been the day before, to see her. She'd get the oats and dried apples first. Slipping quietly along the side of the dugout, she listened for signs of Mrs. Swathmore. Sure enough, she was stretched out on the feather bed, fast asleep, the baby beside her.

The kitchen area was already a mess. Tin plates were piled in a bucket waiting to be washed. The oats and dried apples were where she had left them. In spite of her very great care to be soundless, a tin plate fell to the floor. Mrs. Swathmore stirred. The baby began crying. "Oh my head," Mrs. Swathmore moaned, "Shut up your cryin' face!" Grace froze. Mrs. Swathmore sat up, back to her, reaching for the baby. "A body can't have a minute's peace." Holding her breath, Grace slipped out, rags tied up with oats and dried apples in hand. The little ones were still at play on the wagon.

She ran to the lean-to, collecting her father's things. Just as she was about to step back out she heard loud voices. It was Junior and Ruby quarreling. It was clear that they'd been sent back. Grace cowered behind the pile of hay in the lean-to, hoping they would go inside the dugout. But they didn't. The quarrel ended as they came into the lean-to and threw themselves on the hay, panting.

"Pa said Grace is headin' for the tradin' post," said Junior after awhile.

"Reckon she'll get there?" asked Ruby.

"Nah, she's too dumb. Pa'll find her."

"Reckon I'd like to run away," said Ruby.

"What fer?" Junior asked.

"Just to see if I could do it," laughed Ruby.

"If I was to run away, I'd get me a magic lamp like Aladdin," said Junior.

"Where'd you find a lamp like that?" scoffed Ruby. "I'd rob me a bank. Then I'd have all the money I wanted."

Grace was trapped. She felt sure Old Shep would stay where she told him, but waiting it out while the twins lolled about on the hay was losing her precious minutes. Usually on the run, the twins seemed worn out and lay in the hay, not quite awake and not fully asleep. After what seemed forever, Ruby said, "Reckon what there is to eat?" They raced to the dugout. Stiff from crouching in one position for so long, Grace slipped out of the lean-to and crept around behind it where she could see across the meadow to the creek. She hadn't thought through how she would carry the oats and dried apples and she couldn't risk going back to look for something. In desperation she rolled them up in her skirt, securing it around her waist with her sash. Running for her life was hardly the time to worry about her tatty petticoat showing.

The oxen and milk cow were grazing nearby. They looked at her placidly. The late afternoon sun had already started to drop toward the West. It was still early for milking. Looking both ways, she darted to where the gentle, friendly beasts stood. Keeping them between herself and the dugout, she spoke softly to them. They returned to their grazing. Before she could make a dash for the creek, Mr. Swathmore appeared, carrying a couple of dead animals, a grim reminder of his traps. Grace huddled behind the oxen, praying he wouldn't look their way. She needn't have worried. He dropped the animals by the lean-to and headed to the dugout. "You'd better not be in that bed when I get in there, Mrs.," he yelled. "Fetch me something to eat. Reckon that girl has outsmarted the lot of us and headed north. She can't hold out long. I've a mind to let her starve to death, but we need the help. I'm goin' after her."

There was no time to lose. As soon as he was out of sight, Grace fled for the creek. She stopped just long enough to fill the tin canteen, crouched behind some brush. Then she carefully picked her way up the far bank where Old Shep waited. They could follow the creek all the way to the Cimarron. After that, she wasn't sure. It had been months since they had come that way in the wagon. It wouldn't be easy to retrace their path. But it was all she knew to do. Old Shep had found her before when the wagon was several days from the trail. Surely he could help her find the way back.

They spent the night huddled in a hollow place among sandstone rocks near the creek. Grace crunched on a few oats, dried apple, and some wild greens. She wasn't sure what Old Shep found to eat. She was terrified that Mr. Swathmore would find them, but Old Shep kept watch through the night.

She woke up stiff and cold. They followed the creek, staying above the water line to avoid traps. Old Shep led the way. That night she dug a fire pit in the dark, using a sharp rock. It wasn't perfect, but it worked. She made a fire with her father's flint rock and steel. She didn't cook anything, she didn't have a cooking pot, but they slept close to the fire. It was surprisingly chilly along the creek at night. She covered the pit before dawn, remembering Mr. Payne's advice.

Chapter 13

By the third day out, Grace wondered how close behind Mr. Swathmore was. Old Shep seemed to know. She was almost frantic, fearful of being caught, fearful that if they weren't caught they'd die in the wilderness.

Her feet were in terrible shape, cut and bleeding. When she was sure that she couldn't go on, Old Shep took charge, nuzzling her until she got up. All day, when Grace wanted to stop, he wouldn't let her, nudging her with his nose, even nipping at her until she went on. Sometimes he stopped and lay down. Grace fell down beside him until he was up and off again. She knew that Mr. Swathmore was never far behind.

Chapter 14

THE MAN IN THE DREAM

When Old Shep woke her on the fourth day, Grace could barely get up. "We just have to keep on till we get to the Cimarron, Old Shep," she said, wondering if they would be caught before they reached it. The last light of sunset was giving away to dark when they reached the banks of the river. Grace's heart sank. The Cimarron was running high, higher than she expected. They wouldn't be able to cross where the wagon had crossed early that spring. They'd have to follow it north and hope for a better crossing. Then they'd have to find the Santa Fe Trail somewhere across the vast prairie that stood between. She was already weak, nearly perishing from hunger. She gnawed on oats. The dried apple was long gone and there was no time to forage for edible plants. Old Shep must be nearly starving, she hadn't seen him eat anything. She was confident Mr. Swathmore was still following. He wouldn't give up so easily, not when he trapped all the way to the Cimarron.

They'd have to head north cautiously, getting started before daylight. There wouldn't be time to leave a false trail. Every minute counted. She tried digging a fire pit, but the soil was too sandy. She fell asleep cold and exhausted.

Well before dawn began reaching toward the horizon, a loud snap and the painful cry of an animal startled Grace awake. Old Shep bristled. Upwind a few yards away, was a trap they had barely missed when they settled for the night. A raccoon was not so lucky. It's front paw was locked in cruel steel jaws.

"Quiet, Old Shep. We mustn't frighten it more." Grace walked slowly toward the raccoon. "Let me help you, Raccoon. I think I can undo that trap if you'll let me." Grace spoke quietly. She knew they needed to be off, but she couldn't bear to leave an animal suffering.

The raccoon snarled, teeth bared. Old Shep stayed a respectful distance away.

"Come, come Friend Raccoon, she's only trying to help." Grace heard a friendly voice before she saw a very tall man stepping out from behind the trees. At first she thought he might be from one of the tribes living in Oklahoma Territory, since he wore unfringed buckskins. But his short silver-gray hair and well-trimmed beard gave him away. He looked like the angel in her dream. *Maybe I'm still dreaming, she thought. If it were only a dream and I could wake up in my four-poster bed in St. Louis with Mamma cooking breakfast!*

It was no dream. Old Shep jumped up and down with excitement. He greeted the man as if he were a long lost friend, wagging all over and licking an outstretched hand.

"Hello, Old Shep," said the man in a low voice. "I think we can help Friend Raccoon if we work together, Grace, but we'll have to be quick. The owner of these traps will be along soon. I think you would not like to be found here."

Grace looked into kind eyes. *How does he know my name?*

The raccoon quit snarling at the sound of the man's voice. It stood obediently as he forced the trap open. Following the man's directions, Grace carefully freed the raccoon's paw. Old Shep watched as if the whole rescue operation were his idea.

The man removed a small pouch from the large canvas bag he carried across his shoulder and rubbed something on the raccoon's paw. "Your paw will be tender for awhile, Friend, but it should mend nicely. It's a miracle it isn't broken. I'm sorry, but I can't make these traps go away. You must promise to be more careful in the future—tell your family, too."

The raccoon looked at him for a moment, then limped away.

Turning to Grace, the man said, "Follow me."

Without question she followed. Walking quickly, he led back upstream to where the narrow trunk of a fallen tree spanned the creek banks. Muddy red water boiled below in a rush to meet the Cimarron. The man walked across as light footed as the circus acrobats Grace had read about in days long since gone. The creek was deep and narrow at this point. Even in full daylight, with Mr. Swathmore on her heels, Grace wouldn't have risked such a crossing. She gulped, frozen. "Come," said the man. She stepped cautiously, feeling the rough bark underfoot, damp, but not slippery. "Look at me. Don't look down."

She took a deep breath, fixing her eyes on the man. She didn't waver, or look down, or fall until she reached the far bank, stumbling as the man grasped her hands, helping her to the welcome ground. Old Shep trotted lightly across, leaping to the bank. Once through the woods along the creek, they stepped into a meadow where a magnificent, untethered dun horse grazed in the pre-dawn light. His deep tan coat, black mane, tail, and legs glistened in the sun. Lifting his graceful head, the horse came to them, black ears pointed forward.

"I have found Grace, Song of the Wind," said the man. "We must be on our way." The horse looked at her with curiosity. Nickering softly, he touched noses with Old Shep. Obviously, they knew each other, too.

The man did not saddle the horse, but offered his hand to help Grace mount. "Song of the Wind will carry you. Don't worry, he will take care of you." Reaching into his bag, he pulled out something that looked like corncakes, giving one to Grace and one to Old Shep. The cake was full of seeds, sweet, but not too sweet. He handed her a small, lightweight woolen blanket to wrap around herself.

After they had walked briskly for about fifteen minutes or so, the man rode, too. Seated behind him, Grace felt safe for the first time since the Swathmores took her.

Song of the Wind followed the Cimarron south at a slow, steady trot. The man alternated riding and walking until almost noon. They stopped beside another, smaller creek that cut its way through the low hills to join the Cimarron. "I think we're well out of danger now, Grace. We'll give Song of the Wind and Old Shep a rest. I need a stretch, how about you?"

Unaccustomed to riding, Grace was stiff. Her knees and legs ached. It was torture to walk. She stretched, picking wild flowers while the man gave Song of the Wind a handful of grain.

Shyly giving him the flowers, she asked, "What should I call you, Sir?"

"What would you like to call me?" he asked, sitting down on a large rock in the shade. There was a merry twinkle in his eyes.

"Your name, Sir."

He laughed a hearty, jolly laugh. "I have several names. They're rather complicated. Perhaps you can think of a good one."

"Are you Saint Nicholas?" Grace asked on an impulse. Something about his kind, deep-down joyful manner made her think of Christmas.

"No, but I accept the compliment," he said, fishing more of the seed cakes out of his bag. "It isn't a bad name, either. How about Nichols? Would that suit?"

"Yes," said Grace. "Mr. Nichols. It's not quite Saint Nicholas, but almost."

"Then Mr. Nichols it is."

"How do you know my name?" Grace wanted to know.

"To make a very long story short, some years ago Old Shep broke his leg. I was in a bit of a jam. They didn't know me any better than you do right now, but your mamma and daddy took Old Shep in without question. You were a little tot then. I think Old Shep made it his special business to look after you. In fact, it was his idea to return to St. Louis before you left. A good thing, too."

Old Shep, stretched out in the shade, lifted his head and looked their way. He had a satisfied expression on his face.

"You are Mr. C'lestin. That's why Old Shep knows you!" Grace exclaimed. "Daddy said you were an unusual and mysterious person, but nice."

"I suppose I am unusual," said Mr. Nichols, eyes twinkling. "I have been known to be mysterious, and I try to be nice." He laughed a jolly, musical laugh.

"Do you mind if I still call you Mr. Nichols?"

"Not at all," he said. "In fact, I think it is a very good idea."

"Are you the person who's been tampering with Mr. Swathmore's traps?"

"Sometimes, when I have an opportunity. You know, even small acts of kindness are important. It was important to our raccoon friend that we free her paw. I was actually looking for you. You see, Old Shep came for me the night the Swathmores took you. I'm so sorry, Grace, but by the time we got to them, your father was dead and your mother was very, very sick.

"Your mamma and daddy worked themselves nearly to death helping other members of the train. Your mother had been without water too long in her weakened condition when we got to her. The pox got the upper hand."

Grace had not allowed herself to think that Mamma and Daddy really were dead. Her eyes filled with tears, but she didn't cry. She had stored up about all the tears a person can cry in a lifetime, yet somehow they wouldn't come out.

Mr. Nichols gave her his big pocket-handkerchief. "Some things are worth crying about, Grace. Just when you think you've cried all your tears, you find there are more. I can't think of anything worse than losing your parents. Your mother and daddy loved you very much."

"Mamma said Daddy couldn't get smallpox," Grace injected. "He had it when he was a boy."

"He didn't die of smallpox, Grace. Mr. Swathmore came in the night and stabbed your daddy and Jim Payne in the back. The Swathmores kidnapped you and stole the wagon. Your mamma saw it all, but she was too weak to stop them. They left her on the road next to your daddy's body, where I found her. I promised her I would find you and take you back to your grandparents in St. Louis. She was able to die at peace."

"You mean Mamma didn't ask the Swathmores to take care of me?"

"Absolutely not. She would never have left you with such miserable excuses for human beings. Mr. Swathmore stole everything your family owned except your Daddy's precious collection of medical books and the boxes of medical supplies. I rescued those things and took them back as far as Council Grove where they went out with the next train. I sent them to a retired army doctor in California. They'll go on to help do what your mamma and daddy didn't get to do."

"I knew they were bad, but I didn't think the Swathmores were so very bad as that," said Grace.

"I sent Old Shep after you and stayed with your mother until she died. I knew Old Shep would take care of you. I didn't come for you as soon as I'd hoped. I'm sorry that I didn't get to you before those ruffians tore up the dugout. You may be interested to know that I arranged for Leon and Dillan to meet a very fine U.S. Marshall who was happy to see them."

Before they rode on, Mr. Nichols had her wash her feet and legs thoroughly in the Cimarron. He gave her some of the ointment from his pouch to put on the cuts and scratches. She didn't need the blanket around her now. He folded it for her to sit on. "It takes a while to get used to riding. Song of the Wind makes it as easy as he can."

Late that afternoon, the Cimarron grew wide and shallower. Even so, crossing it would have been terrifying if Mr. Nichols hadn't promised that Song of the Wind wouldn't let her fall. Song of the Wind looked at her with an expression of patient tolerance as they waited for Mr. Nichols and Old Shep to swim across. After Song of the

Wind reached the far bank, Grace slid off. She thanked him. Song of the Wind rewarded her with a soft nicker.

When Grace worried that his wet buckskin shirt and trousers would shrink in the hot sun, Mr. Nichols laughed. "This only looks like buckskin. I like for animals to keep their own hides. So do they!"

They found a grove of trees well before sundown. Mr. Nichols said it would be a good place to camp. "Song of the Wind needs a good rest."

Grace asked if he wanted her to make a pit fire. He was impressed.

"Mr. Payne taught me." She suddenly felt a catch in her throat.

"He was a good man, Grace," said Mr. Nichols. "He left a wife and three children. Mrs. Payne decided to turn back once news reached the wagon train. I accompanied her back to Council Grove when I took your daddy's books and supplies."

"She won't get to start a school in California," said Grace sadly.

"Oh, but I think she will. She's a strong woman. She wanted to see where Jim Payne was buried. Then she and the children joined the next train out of Council Grove. They're already in California. She saw that the medical books and supplies got to the right place, too."

"Maybe I'll go to California when I grow up," Grace said hopefully. "If Mrs. Payne can do it, so can I."

"You might just do that. A lot of folk told Mrs. Payne that she couldn't go to California without a man to look after her, but she did it anyway."

The next morning, Mr. Nichols handed her a pair of woolen moccasins. He'd made them from his blanket. "They won't last very long, but they are better than nothing," he said.

Days fell into a pattern of getting up before dawn, eating breakfast—Song of the Wind had grain, everyone else had seed cake—walking until Song of the Wind warmed up, then alternating between riding and walking. They took rest breaks and a long stop around noon to give Song of the Wind time to graze. For the most part, they passed through a deserted land of low hills, valleys with tree lined creeks or rivers, and a vast, never-ending horizon. Occasionally they saw buffalo.

One evening while they made camp, Grace asked, "How old is Old Shep?"

"Old enough," said Mr. Nichols.

"No, I mean, how long has he been alive?"

"Why do you ask?"

"Well, when he came to us the day before the auction, Mamma said he couldn't be Old Shep.

He'd be one hundred three in doggie years. Then Daddy said they must have got his age wrong."

"Old Shep and I don't measure age in years," said Mr. Nichols.

"Is he magic?" asked Grace.

"Of course he is," said Mr. Nichols. "And so are you. We all have a little magic in us, don't you think?"

It wasn't a very satisfying answer. Her Daddy was right. Mr. Nichols was a mysterious person.

Once Mr. Nichols brought them all to a halt. "This is something to see," he said. It was a buffalo hunt. From their far-away hill they watched as Niukonska [Ni-u-kon-ska] hunters picked off buffalo from a stampeding herd. "French explorers called them Osage Indians. They never kill more than they need," he said. "That is how it should be."

Another time, during a break, Grace asked, "What will happen to Mr. and Mrs. Swathmore?"

"I don't know," said Mr. Nichols. "The way I see it, having to live with themselves is punishment enough for people like the Swathmores."

"But Old Shep?" Grace was perplexed. "Why couldn't Old Shep keep it from happening—if he's magic."

"Old Shep and I don't keep things from happening, Grace. We can only help you with what happens."

One morning Mr. Nichols pointed toward the sunrise, "Can you see the trees just there on the horizon? That is the Missouri River. We'll be in Kansas City before you know it."

Chapter 15

A CHANGE OF PLANS

When Grace saw the bathtub in their hotel rooms in Kansas City, she could hardly believe it. She hadn't had a bath in an actual bathtub since before the wagon train set out for Santa Fe. Mr. Nichols said he was going out to get a bath, haircut, and shave. He'd send a maid up to help her.

Grace wasn't used to having help, at least not since she was kidnapped. It was very nice to have someone else fill the tub with hot water. She thanked the maid, whose name was Rosy. After a long soak in the tub, Rosy brought her a warm towel. Waiting on her bed when she dried off, was a box that held two brand new dresses, petticoats, underwear, shoes, a nightgown and everything a girl needed to feel well dressed.

A note from Mr. Nichols said, "Let's treat ourselves to a lemonade. I will be in the lobby."

She chose a dress in blue cotton, made with yards and yards of fabric. It had long puffy sleeves and buttons down the back, but no annoying frills. Rosy did the buttons in the back for her and tied a matching ribbon in her hair. "Now don't you look pretty, Missy!" said Rosy, beaming.

"Where are my old clothes?" Grace asked, admiring herself in the mirror.

"Your Grandpa said to throw them away," said Rosy.

"Oh no!" Grace cried. "My handkerchief."

"I didn't see no hankie, Missy."

Grace ran to the trashcan and began shaking out her old clothes. They were tattered and dirty. The handkerchief was at the bottom of the heap. "My Grandma made this for me," she explained.

"It's beautiful, Missy," said Rosy. "I'll wash it out for you. It will do up real nice."

Grace felt like a princess as she hurried downstairs. She could see Mr. Nichols sitting in an obscure corner of the lobby reading a newspaper. He was wearing a suit. His hair and beard had been trimmed.

Just then a woman entered the hotel. She was absolutely the most beautiful woman Grace had ever seen. Behind her was a porter carrying a stack of luggage. Behind him, a nattily dressed man hurried to catch up. The lady was wearing a fashionable maroon travel dress with a matching paisley Indian shawl. Society ladies in St. Louis wore shawls like that. A straw hat with a wide maroon ribbon sat atop a mound of shining hair. Everyone in the lobby stopped in their tracks. Grace tried not to stare, but she couldn't help looking. The clerk at the desk stammered, "May I help you Madame?"

"I believe that arrangements were made for a suite of rooms," she said haughtily.

The manager appeared. "Miss Celeste, I presume. May I show you the rooms?"

"Ainsley, see if the rooms are suitable," the lady directed arrogantly.

Ainsley, the dapper man accompanying Miss Celeste, went with the manager. Behind Ainsley, a plain, primly dressed young woman followed, carrying hat boxes.

"This is the best hotel in Kansas City, Miss," said the clerk. "You won't find better."

"Not here, I daresay. One hardly expects it. This isn't Europe, after all." Miss Celeste turned away, seating herself at one of the little tea tables in the small lobby. Grace couldn't help noticing that despite her seeming indifference and haughty manner, the lady positioned herself where she could be admired to the greatest advantage. Nobody could walk past without seeing her. Everybody who passed stopped and looked, some quietly and inconspicuously, others just out and out gawked.

The manager ordered a lemonade to be sent to Miss Celeste. She demurely sipped it as Ainsley and the maid trotted behind the clerk to inspect the rooms.

Mr. Nichols was lost behind his newspaper, oblivious to everything going on around him. Grace walked around the edges of the lounge so as not to pass in front of the lady. She seated herself in the chair next to Mr. Nichols, quietly waiting for him to finish what he was reading. Without looking out from behind his paper, he said, "There's a book for you in my bag. I want to finish this article. Then we'll get some lemonade."

Grace eagerly found the book. She hadn't had a book of her own since the Swathmores stole the wagon. But she watched the lady out of a corner of her eye. Ainsley returned, saying the rooms would do. Miss Celeste haughtily waved for the men with the bags and trunk to go on ahead and ready the rooms. Ainsley led the way, returning for Miss Celeste several minutes later. She left her place in the center of attention, going upstairs. Her audience of admirers returned to whatever they'd been doing before.

Mr. Nichols' head came out from behind the paper. "Shall we get that lemonade?"

"Did you see that beautiful lady?" Grace asked, marking the place in her book.

"The world is full of ladies who are pretty on the outside," said Mr. Nichols. "I'm more interested in ladies who are pretty inside."

"Maybe this lady is pretty on the inside, too," said Grace, though there was something in the lady's manner that made her rather doubt it.

"Speaking of pretty ladies," said Mr. Nichols, "the dress suits you. I thought you'd like it."

Over lemonade and cookies, he said, "Grace, we were supposed to leave for St. Louis by stagecoach first thing in the morning. But something has happened. I need to go into Oklahoma Territory again. Unfortunately I can't afford to wait until I return from St. Louis. I can see two ways to deal with this. I can put you in the charge of a very kind family who will be on the same stage. It's a long ride, but you could do it without me as long as there's somebody to look after you and see that you get to your grandparents safely. They'll be glad to do that. As soon as I finish my business, I'll come to see you in St. Louis."

Grace took in a sharp breath. But she didn't say anything.

Mr. Nichols continued, "Or, I can arrange for you to stay with a family here in Kansas City until I return. I know a family who will take good care of you. Then I will accompany you to St. Louis. I know you're eager to be back with your grandparents. Regrettably, I can't delay. I wish it were otherwise."

Grace was silent. She looked down at her lemonade.

"I think the second choice is best. There are children in the family, so there will be somebody to play with. Nice children, not at all like Ruby and Junior. What do you think? We can do it either way."

Grace didn't have to think twice. "May I go with you? Please?"

Mr. Nichols thought for a moment. "Grace, it's a long trip, longer than our trip from the Cimarron River to Kansas City. The only way to do it is on horseback. It's risky. I'm not sure what we will encounter. I promised your mother I'd see that you get back to St. Louis safely. I couldn't forgive myself if anything happened to you. I'll visit you in St. Louis as soon as my business is done. It's a promise."

Grace, who'd been unable to cry, suddenly found that sheets of tears were making their way down her face and splashing on to the front of her new dress. Mr. Nichols had rescued her from an unspeakably terrible life. The thought of being with strangers again, no matter how kind they were, was more than she could bear. Now that the tears had started, she couldn't hold them back.

Mr. Nichols understood. "It's been too hard for you, Grace. Probably even harder than I know." Handing her a handkerchief, he thought for a moment. "I'll tell you what, I'll take you with me if you promise to do exactly as I say. I have to be able to count on you. No exceptions."

Grace shook her head yes and blew her nose.

"It will mean the loss of a day," he said, "but I don't think one day will matter that much. I'll have to make some arrangements. We won't be able to stay at the hotel tonight. And you'll have to leave your pretty new dresses behind."

Grace had been looking forward to sleeping in the big featherbed in her room. She wasn't sure why they couldn't stay, but she didn't ask. She loved her new dresses, too, but wearing her old, tattered dress was a small price to pay if it meant she didn't have to stay behind.

"Here's what I need you to do," Mr. Nichols continued. "I'll get our things. You wait for me in that chair right over there in the lounge. You are not to leave it or to talk with anyone, even that pretty lady, if you see her again—especially not the lady."

As Mr. Nichols paid their waiter, he said, "I've left some things upstairs. Would you keep an eye on the little miss for me? She'll be right over there in plain sight. I don't trust everyone who walks past, if you know what I mean." He handed the waiter a gold coin.

"Yes sir," said the waiter, a big grin on his face. "Anybody looks at her cross-eyed will have to answer to me."

While Mr. Nichols went upstairs, Grace sat in the lounge chair reading her book and watching people walk past. Several men and women, all dressed up in evening clothes, paraded down the stairs, through the lounge to the wide front doors where the doorman settled them into carriages. "There must be a big party somewhere," the waiter said. He brought her another lemonade and half a dozen more cookies. "This is from me," he said. "I have a little sister. She likes cookies, too."

Grace didn't even try to tell him how long it had been since she'd had lemonade and cookies. Before long she'd eaten every one and finished off her lemonade.

The lounge was almost empty when Miss Celeste, swept down the stairs on the arm of Ainsley. She wore a magnificent green water-marked taffeta gown. Her hair was swept back, falling in ringlets to her shoulders. "This place is like a ghost town," she said in a very snooty voice as they walked across the lounge.

"It isn't entirely deserted. There's a very pretty little girl over here," said Ainsley, winking at Grace.

Miss Celeste glanced at her with haughty eyes. "I have no interest in children," she said.

"Certainly not one so ordinary." She made no effort to keep her voice down. The words hit Grace like a slap in the face. She quickly looked down at her book. She could feel her face going all hot and red.

"Everyone must already be there. Good," said Miss Celeste. "It will spare us waiting. I can't think why I agreed to something so uncivilized in a place so desolate."

"You'll give these locals something to talk about for years to come," said Ainsley.

"Your carriage, Miss Celeste," said the doorman. "May I say that you look beautiful. . ."

"Yes, yes," Miss Celeste cut him off.

Shortly after, Mr. Nichols returned with a bag and the large box Grace's dresses came in. "Rosy said you would want this." He handed her the handkerchief. Rosy had been right. The handkerchief had "done up" nicely. She tucked it into her wide sash.

"Our plans have changed," Mr. Nichols said to the hotel clerk. "I'll pay you for the rooms tonight, but we won't be staying over."

"Yes sir," said the clerk as Mr. Nichols paid their bill.

That night they stayed with a family Mr. Nichols knew who let rooms. "They know me as Mr. Bright," explained Mr. Nichols. "If you call me Mr. Nichols, they will be all confused." The next morning, he gave her strict orders to say nothing about where they'd been or where they were going, leaving her in the care of the family. The children were busy with chores all morning. Grace was content to read her book. In the afternoon she played hop scotch and hide and seek with them. It reminded her of good times with Sid Johnson.

Sadness welled up as she remembered Sid. Mamma said that things don't always come out the way we want them to. Nothing seemed to be coming out right.

When Mr. Nichols returned it was too late in the day for them to leave. After supper, when they'd returned to their rooms, he laid a package on Grace's bed. "More clothes—not quite new, I confess."

In the package were knee pants, a shirt, vest, jacket, stockings, boots and a large cap. "You will be much safer dressed as a boy," Mr. Nichols said. "I'm sorry they aren't new, but they're clean. New clothes would make you stand out. That's the last thing we want." Then he took a big pair of scissors and cut Grace's hair to just even with her chin, "I think we can get away with that. I hate to cut it all off." Looking at her, he laughed, "Now you look a bit more like your Daddy." He gathered up the shorn locks of hair. Wrapping them in paper, he put them in his bag. "We won't leave this here for someone to find.

We don't need questions or to leave anybody wondering. In the morning you'll need to keep your bonnet on and wrap this blanket around you. I don't want to risk anybody in the family seeing you dressed as a boy and asking more questions. They had more than enough questions at supper."

Grace tried on the clothes, studying herself in the mirror. She did look a bit like her Daddy.

"We'll leave your dresses and nightgown here," said Mr. Nichols. "They'll keep a box for us until our return." Grace hadn't thought the dresses meant so much to her until he said that. She'd outgrown the two dresses she'd worn on the Santa Fe Trail. They were shabby from the wear and tear of her hard life with the Swathmores. Everything else packed for Grace to have in California had been given to Ruby. The dress she was wearing when she ran away was in tatters. Mr. Nichols was right to have Rosy throw it away.

They were on their way well before breakfast the next morning. Mr. Nichols wore trousers and a shirt like men on the Santa Fe Trail. Grace was wrapped in her blanket, but nobody saw them slip out. Song of the Wind and a painted pony were waiting in the barn. The pony was white with brown patches. "He's sweet tempered and almost as fast as Song of the Wind. His name is Patches," said Mr. Nichols.

"What about Old Shep?" asked Grace.

"What do you think, Old Shep?" asked Mr. Nichols. Old Shep had been sleeping in the barn with the horses. "It's going to be a long, fast journey. Are your ready for it?"

Old Shep gave one short bark. It was settled. He was going, too.

Chapter 16

THE ALABASTER CAVERN

As trips on horseback with sleeping on the ground go, it wasn't too difficult. Patches was the best of ponies. Grace was glad to ride astride and not sidesaddle as women often did. She was also glad that a dress and petticoats didn't hamper her.

They stopped along the trail where the Johnson wagon had pulled away from the wagon train. Except for Sid, all of the Johnsons had lived. There was no trace of where Sid had been buried. Just off the trail, Mr. Nichols helped Grace erect a cairn of rocks in his memory.

When they reached the site where her Mamma and Daddy and Jim Payne were buried, Grace helped Mr. Nichols place simple markers. "I wish these were in bronze, but I'm afraid there are some who would even steal a grave marker," he said.

Grace picked wild flowers and scattered them on the graves. Some feelings are too deep to put into words. She sat by their graves in silence for a long time.

Mr. Nichols didn't rush her. They spent the night there.

"Your Mamma and Daddy were good people, Grace," said Mr. Nichols as they made ready to leave the next morning. "Your Daddy helped anybody who needed a doctor. It didn't matter if they couldn't pay or if other people thought they weren't worth helping. And your Mamma was one of those rare people who is pretty on the inside and outside."

Tears ran down Grace's face as she took a last look at the graves. "Mr. Payne was a good man, too. He taught me how to be a scout."

"He was indeed," said Mr. Nichols. "He didn't know it, but he probably saved your life. What he taught you made it hard for Mr. Swathmore to track you when you escaped."

Old Shep, Patches, and Song of the Wind were waiting. They left in silence.

A few days later, they were well into Oklahoma Territory, following a path similar to that Mr. Swathmore had taken. The low, rolling hills covered with prairie grass looked familiar. Creeks cut through the valleys. Most of the creeks beds were dry and covered with red dirt and rocks, now that summer was coming to an end.

"Thousands of years ago this was one vast inland sea," Mr. Nichols explained. It almost looked like the sea with the prairie grasses rippled by the wind.

They came upon a wide canyon one afternoon. Grace remembered the white patches of gypsum rock that dotted the short, gray-green buffalo grass around them. She passed by scenes like this in the Swathmore wagon. The red dirt walls of the canyon were a sharp contrast to the white rock and dark green of cedar trees growing everywhere.

Mr. Nichols pointed to a massive cliff with a thick grove of cottonwood trees and brush growing at the bottom. "There is a vast network of caverns under all this land. They probably won't be discovered for another twenty years or so. It would make a great hide-out for robbers."

Grace wanted to ask how he knew all of these things. But something held her back.

They let Song of the Wind take the lead in finding a way down into the canyon below. Patches followed with Old Shep bringing up the rear. Then they dismounted, leaving Song of the Wind and Patches to graze.

Behind the thick growth at the bottom of the canyon was the entrance to a cave, perfectly hidden from view. "You have to know this is here to find it," said Mr. Nichols. Patches of long prairie grass, sagebrush, and plum thickets competed for growing space. Before they entered the cave, Mr. Nichols showed Grace how to twist the long prairie grass into a torch. They made several torches to take inside with them.

"This is where you stay behind, Old Shep. I'm counting on you to let us know if we have any unexpected company." Old Shep wagged his tail and nodded knowingly. Grace gave him a hug around the neck. He rewarded her with a doggie kiss.

"You might say this is where things get mysterious," said Mr. Nichols. "Stay close behind me. Don't step to the right or left until we have some light." Once inside he struck a flint rock and lit a torch. They made their way down a natural rock stairway. The footing was uneven. They went slowly until they were well inside a huge cavern. The floor was strewn with rock piles and large boulders. The walls picked up the light of the torch and sent it back in a thousand shining lights. Grace had never seen, nor had she imagined such a place. It was beautiful and frightening at the same time. Without Mr. Nichols, she would be hopelessly lost.

"This is all pure alabaster, studded with crystal," he said. They wound through narrow passages into several smaller rooms, crossing natural bridges. Water rushed along somewhere below, just out of sight. "That is pure black alabaster," he said, holding the torch up to let the light hit a dark streak that cut through the pink. "There are only a couple of other places in the world where you find black alabaster, China and Italy."

China and Italy. To Grace they were only names of far-away places in a geography book. "How do you know so much?" she could no longer hold the question back.

"I've been around for a long, long time," he said.

It wasn't a satisfying answer, but he said no more.

At last they came to a room where pink alabaster and crystals shone like diamonds. Grace felt as if she had entered fairyland. It was breathtaking. A natural rock bridge, studded with alabaster and crystal made an arch over a stream that divided the vast room in half. At the far end, across the stream, a large block of unpolished black alabaster stood like an ancient cairn marking something of importance. On top of it was a large polished, black alabaster stone, squared off like a box.

"So it is still here," said Mr. Nichols, more to himself than to Grace. "I didn't think it had been removed, but I couldn't take the risk."

"People have been here before?" asked Grace.

"There was someone here, a long, long time ago." Mr. Nichols said. "One of these days she will return. She doesn't need what's inside that box yet, but this wild and free piece of the earth is becoming settled. She won't want anyone else finding the Alabaster Box." Sighing, he anchored one of the torches in the rocks. "I feared that might explain her sudden appearance," he said, again, almost to himself.

He spread a blanket on some large rocks. "We shall sit for awhile. I must think."

They sat looking across at the box for a very long time. Their torch was nearly gone. Grace quietly replaced it. Still he didn't move. While he thought, Grace looked at the crystal and imagined shapes of things and patterns. It was like cloud gazing.

At last he said, "There are at least two other boxes inside the Alabaster Box. They are guarding a crystal. Let me see, how do I explain this without keeping us here for days and days." He thought for a moment.

"You see, Grace, when the Earth was born, Immortals wandered about freely as did the Angels. They delighted in each new living thing, tending the Earth like a garden. But, as the Earth grew older, Mortals came. Immortals watched as people spread over all of the Earth, using it as if there would always be some fresh, new place to spoil. Forests were lost. Mountains cut down, great gashes left in the Earth. The powerful used the meek and lowly as if their lives were of no consequence. Mortal fought against Mortal to own what was never theirs, bringing death and leaving a burned, scarred land. The Immortals who had lovingly tended the earth were distressed to leave it in such hands, yet their time was drawing to an end.

"It so happened that in the days when the Earth was young, a cold, clear fountain of water stood high upon the back of the tallest mountain in the great North. In its depths seven crystals grew. Sealed within each was water from the day the Earth was made. Water of a Thousand Lights, rich, life-renewing water.

"The Immortals said to each other, 'Pour out water from the crystals when the Earth seems torn and spent. It will heal where the Earth is hurt. It will build where the Earth is broken. It will repair where the Earth is rent. As the Earth blossoms, so will its people. Wars will cease. Kindness will reign with justice and compassion as her partners.'" Mr. Nichols paused.

"Is that what the crystal inside the boxes is for?" asked Grace, eager to learn more.

"Yes, to heal and repair the Earth," Mr. Nichols said.

"So are we going to get it to heal and repair the Earth?"

"I wish we could. The earth needs healing," he sighed again. "Unfortunately, I am prevented from doing so. When the day came for the first crystal to be broken for the healing of the Earth, it was no longer in the fountain pool. Nor were any left there. They had all been stolen."

"Stolen?"

"It was given to Immortal Twins, born the day the Earth was made, to care for the crystals and to decide when Mother Earth needed them. At first, the Twins used their powers to do great good. But Celeste, the firstborn, became distracted by the ways of Mortals. She saw how mortal women made themselves beautiful and longed to be the most beautiful woman on Earth. So she began to work in darkness. Studying with a great and evil sorcerer, she secretly became even more powerful than her brother. Unbeknownst to him, she bound the crystals to herself with the darkest of dark magic, hiding them over the earth where only she could claim them. She was very, very powerful then. But there was a price to be paid in exchange for the dark magic. She had to give up her immortality. When she became a Mortal, she lost all of her magical powers. But the powers binding the crystals remained for she wove those powers into the spell that held them.

"Since then, she has chosen to live among the people of earth as one of them. One by one she has used the crystals to stay young and beautiful. Now only this one remains. It is the Last Crystal. Since then, the Earth has reeled in pain. War has followed war until the bones of men pile high. Hate and prejudice blind the hearts of men and women to love. Greed is rampant. The Earth needs a blossoming of compassion and kindness and goodness. Yet, I am powerless to intervene."

Chapter 16

"You are C'lestin. Celeste's twin," Grace said, struggling to grasp the enormity of what she was saying.

Mr. Nichols got up and lit another torch. "I come to check on this last crystal occasionally. This is where Old Shep found me the night your mother died."

"So there is such a thing as magic," Grace said, almost to herself.

"Oh yes," he sighed. "I sit before this crystal as I have sat before the others. I still hold out hope that there will be a way to claim it for its intended use. But as the Earth has passed from her youth to full maturity, I have not yet found a way to undo the magic that holds even one of the crystals."

"Undo the magic?" asked Grace.

"Yes, usually there's a way around such magic. But the magic wrapped around that Alabaster Box is such that neither Angel, nor Immortal, nor Mortal Man, nor Beast may open it—only Celeste. If I tried, I wouldn't even be able to open the lid. If, by some chance I did, all sorts of horrors would be unleashed on us and on the world. I am powerless." Mr. Nichols sounded tired and sad. "She is the only one who can unlock it. And much as I wish otherwise, her heart will not change."

They sat in silence again for a long time. Mr. Nichol's head was bowed.

"Neither Angel, nor Immortal, nor Mortal Man, nor Beast?" repeated Grace softly, looking up at the alabaster ceiling. "Does that mean Mortal Woman, too?"

Mr. Nichols looked up, startled by her question. "Why yes, child. Mortal Man means all of humankind, men and women."

"But what about a child? It doesn't say child. Maybe I could get it for you."

Mr. Nichols looked at her in wonder. "Let me think on this. The spells binding the crystals were in an ancient language. When we say man or humankind we mean any person regardless of age or whether that person is male or female. But in the original language. . ." His voice trailed off as he sat thinking. Suddenly his face lit up in an enormous smile. "Grace! You just may have it. It wouldn't do to make a mistake, though. I must think this through."

Chapter 17

FACING THE DARK MAGIC

Mr. Nichols sat in a posture of meditation again, this time for so long Grace began to wonder if he'd fallen asleep. Their last torch was beginning to flicker and would soon go out.

At last he stirred. "We will go. Perhaps we shall return tomorrow."

They made their way back in silence. The torch went out long before they reached the entrance to the cave. They were in the darkest dark she had ever known, but Mr. Nichols knew the way. Grace followed, holding to his shirt so she wouldn't get lost or fall into one of the deep fissures that ran through the cave.

Old Shep was waiting for them, stretched across the entrance like a rug. They led the horses to a stream in silence. They made no fire that night, eating the seed bread Mr. Nichols carried with him in silence. Long after Grace rolled up in her bedroll and slept, Mr. Nichols sat up pondering.

"Yes, you could," he said, the next morning when she awoke. He was sitting in the same position he'd been in when she fell asleep. Grace wondered if he'd slept at all.

"But if you do, you will be taking on a burden so heavy that even I do not know its weight."

"Is the crystal really big?" Grace wondered.

Mr. Nichols gave her a sad smile. "No, the crystal itself is very light. The weight is in what may be required of the child who takes it. You see, once the lady knows you have taken it, you will never again be safe. She will want it back."

"But can't I take it and use it to heal the earth? Then she can't get it again."

"No child," Mr. Nichols sighed. "I wish it were that easy. Opening the box is one thing. But whoever breaks the seal of evil magic that binds the crystal to her, will do so at a price—a price that is too high for you to pay. That, I know with certainty."

"Then we can't do anything?" cried Grace.

"We can't do everything, but we can do something. There are three boxes. The shiny one at the top of the cairn is the first box. If you remove the two boxes inside the Alabaster Box, we can save the crystal. That would give me a chance to study the magic that governs these boxes more closely. But we must be careful. If you decide to do this, you will have to do it by yourself. I cannot assist you. And you must promise me that you will never, never, ever try to look at the crystal by yourself or allow anyone to open the boxes holding it."

Grace couldn't even imagine wanting to look at something so dangerous. It was easy to promise. She wanted more than anything to help Mr. Nichols. He had saved her from an unspeakable life. And the thought of doing something good for the earth was compelling. She was glad when he said they would go back into the cave.

"Now Grace," said Mr. Nichols when they were in the crystal room, "You will have to walk over the bridge alone. You must open the Alabaster Box slowly. I don't know exactly what will happen, but I do know that you cannot be harmed. You are not breaking the rules of the magic that bind the box. I am certain of that. I've thought it through from every angle. You will be safe as long as you do not open the last of the nested boxes—the golden box. We have to stay within the boundaries set by the magic. Besides, I'm here."

Grace listened intently, determined not to waver.

"I understand this particular magic enough to know that when you open the Alabaster Box there will be a voice demanding who you are and challenging your right to open it. You see, if you had no right to open it—that is, if you were an Angel, Immortal, Mortal Man or Woman, or Beast—you would die the moment you opened it. So you will be challenged. You must say, 'It is I, a child—neither Angel, Immortal, Mortal Man, nor Beast.' Those are the words of the spell. That is all you are to say. Absolutely nothing else, no matter what the voice says or promises. In fact, it could promise you almost anything, though it will be making false promises. You must have courage and stand firm. Look in the box, but do not look to the right or left. I know this is complicated, but we have to work with the magic, not against it. Understand?"

Grace nodded. She didn't know anything about magic, but she trusted Mr. Nichols.

"Inside the Alabaster Box will be a wooden box with golden hinges. Inside that is a golden box set with jewels. You will need to open the wooden box, and look inside to be sure the golden box is there. *By no means* are you to try to open the golden box."

Grace swallowed nervously. It was beginning to sound scary.

"I don't know enough about it yet," said Mr. Nichols. "It is a magic so powerful I have been unable to restore any of the crystals in all these years. I shall study the magic when you open the boxes. Remember, say nothing more. Do not answer questions. You will probably see a face, or maybe just eyes. They are an illusion, but there is power in them. Do not look directly at the eyes. Look at the nose or the chin if you see a face. Keep looking into the box, not out of the box. Are you with me so far?"

"Yes sir," said Grace, feeling the gravity in his voice. He asked her to repeat the directions.

When he was satisfied, he said, "The face is part of the magic. The eyes allow you to be seen. If you look at them, they will draw you into the magic. If you look anywhere around the cavern, they can see what you are looking at. I do not want the eyes to see me or you will be in greater danger. If this is too frightening, you do not have to do it. It is better to refuse now than to begin and be unable to finish."

"But I want to help," said Grace, more determined than ever.

He looked at her with steady eyes for a moment. "Are you sure?"

"Yes!" she said forcefully. "I want to do this."

"After you see that the golden box is there, close the wooden box. Keep looking down into the Alabaster Box. Lift the wooden box out of the Alabaster Box and set it on this wool blanket. Cover it up with the ends of the blanket, like this." Mr. Nichols placed her cap in the blanket, folding the ends over her cap. "You have to be able to do this without actually looking at what you are doing. Keep looking into the Alabaster

Box, but not the eyes. When the wooden box is securely in the blanket, close the Alabaster Box. If there are any voices or sounds or images that appear when the boxes are open, they will be contained in the boxes when you close them. Leave the Alabaster Box there as you found it. Then hold the blanket at arm's length, don't hold it to your chest." He held the blanket with her cap out to show her. "Bring it back with you like this. While the magic is newly disrupted, I want to be very cautious."

Grace had to review the directions again and practice looking at him while she wrapped her cap in the blanket. Then he put the cap back on her head. "Most of all, Grace, don't be alarmed by anything you see or hear from the boxes. *Anything*. Nothing can harm you because you have not broken the rules of the magic. The voice may be sweet or terrible. But you must not give in to it or do what it tells you to do." Then he reached down and picked up some dirt from the cave floor. "Here, I'm going to smudge your face with dirt so it will be harder for her to see who you are." With that he smeared dirt on her cheeks and across her nose.

Heart pounding with fear and excitement, Grace stood.

"Once you cross that bridge, don't look back at me," said Mr. Nichols. "No matter what happens, don't look back."

Chapter 18

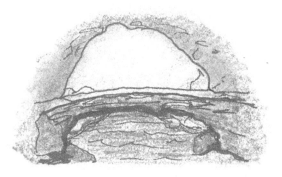

ACROSS THE ALABASTER BRIDGE

Grace was afraid the alabaster bridge would be slippery. It wasn't. When she got to the black alabaster cairn, she could see that the top had been cut away to make a smooth, table-like surface. There was plenty of room for her to spread the blanket beside the Alabaster Box. She practiced lifting an imaginary box from the Alabaster Box and setting it on the cloth without turning her eyes away from the box.

She stood for a moment, gathering courage. The faint light from the torch glistened on the walls. It felt as if Mr. Nichols were bending his mind on the box and on her. She could feel energy like the warmth of the sun coming from him. But she did not look at him.

Carefully, carefully, she opened the lid of the Alabaster Box. It was hinged, standing open by itself. Inside the lid was polished so highly that she could see her own reflection. Eyes appeared on the polished surface, startling her, then a face. It was the beautiful lady she had seen at the hotel. For a minute she was afraid she would be recognized. She dropped her eyes so as not to look into Celeste's eyes.

"Who is this who dares to open my Alabaster Box?" Celeste demanded sternly. "Know you not that it is forbidden?"

"It is I, a child—neither Angel, nor Immortal, nor Mortal Man, nor Beast," said Grace.

Celeste's reflection in the mirrored lid frowned for a moment, then smiled at her, "Oh, a boy! Look at me dear," she said in a soft, sweet voice. Grace looked at Celeste's mouth.

"The box is mine. You may not have it. If you took it, you would be stealing. You wouldn't want to be a thief, now would you?"

Grace felt uncomfortable, straining to avoid looking into the eyes. It was hard not to. She could feel a force pulling at her to look.

"There is something else, dear. I am the one for whom the box is intended. If you take what is mine, you will die because the box is protected by magic more powerful than anything you can imagine." The words were harsh, but the voice was sweet and soothing. "You cannot escape me, young man. Wherever you go I will see you and I will find you. There is no place on this earth you can hide from me. Close the lid and walk away while you can."

All of this continued in the same soft, hypnotic voice. Grace didn't mean to, but before she realized what she was doing, she looked directly into Celeste's eyes. It was like looking into a whirlpool in the Cimarron River. It took every ounce of her strength to keep from being pulled in. She wrenched her eyes away.

There was something else about the look in those eyes. *What is it?* She wasn't remembering too well. She was tired and sleepy, wanting more than anything to look again.

Celeste kept talking. Her voice was like a lullaby, rocking Grace to sleep. "I know your mamma and daddy wouldn't want you to take things that don't belong to you, would they? I know they would not want their boy to die because he made a foolish mistake."

When Celeste said "mamma and daddy," something in Grace snapped. Remembering them momentarily broke the power of the voice. Grace remembered something else, too. Celeste's eyes glinted like Mr. Swathmore's eyes when he'd been drinking too much corn whiskey and wanted to beat her, or like a snake's eyes when it is all coiled up and ready to strike.

Shaking all over, she pulled her eyes away from the powerful reflection in the lid, looking down at the wooden box again. Even looking at Celeste's mouth was dangerous.

I must open the wooden box, she remembered.

"Look at me, dear. I need you to look at me so that I know you are listening. This is very important," Celeste said sweetly.

Grace reached out with both hands, opening the wooden box with the golden hinges. Inside was a beautiful, golden box set with jewels. A magnificent sapphire stood at the center. Celeste's eyes looked at her from the sapphire.

"I see you are a stubborn and stupid little boy," the voice was stern again. "If you open the golden box, you will do so at the cost of your life. It cost a life to bind it shut and it will cost a life to open it. Even when I open it myself it will be at the cost of a life. Is that what you want—to die? Close the boxes. Go home. Don't ever come back here again."

Grace kept looking down, away from the sapphire. Her head wasn't clear. She wanted the voice to go away. It pulled at her. It took almost every ounce of her strength and will to keep from looking at Celeste's eyes in the sapphire and blurting out everything she knew about herself, and about the cavern, and Mr. Nichols. But she didn't.

Celeste spoke in her soft, reassuring voice again, "Why, I think you must be all alone, child.

135

What is your name? Where do you come from?" Grace stood frozen, saying nothing.

"Look at me, child, and be safe. Look at me and you will not remember the box and you will live."

Head in a muddle, Grace was still trembling. *There is something I have to do*, she thought. *What is it I have to do? Something Mamma told me to do. No, it wasn't Mamma. Who told me?* She tried to remember her mother's face. It wasn't Mamma. It was Mr. Nichols. *I must not look. I must shut the lid.* Without looking directly at the eyes in the sapphire, Grace gently closed the lid of the wooden box.

"There's a clever lad," said the soothing voice. "But you haven't answered my questions. I should so much like to know who I am to thank for closing my wooden box."

Grace felt the softness and gentleness of the voice pulling at her again. She tried thinking of her father's face as she lifted the wooden box from the Alabaster Box and set it on the wool blanket. She thought of how Daddy tucked her in that last night in the wagon before he was killed. She began folding the corners of the blanket just as she'd practiced. Celeste's hypnotic voice droned on. She thought of Mamma smiling at her and blowing a kiss from the bed Daddy and Mr. Payne made for her by the wagon. All the while, Grace kept her eyes fixed on the inside of the Alabaster Box.

Celeste pleaded with her to look into her eyes, then ordered her to do so. Gently, but firmly, with all the strength she had left, Grace reached for the lid of the Alabaster Box. But she couldn't find the strength to close it.

Celeste's terrible eyes and voice watched her from the polished lid. "I could use a clever boy like you." Now her voice was all kindness again. It was as smooth as honey when you have a sore throat. "I don't have a boy of my own, you see. Your mother and father must be so proud of you. I should so like to meet them and tell them what a fine young man they have as a son." Grace was frozen again. She felt like a frog she'd seen once on the creek bank. A snake was swaying hypnotically in front of the poor creature. The frog couldn't help itself. She'd thrown a rock at the snake. Startled, it slithered away, freeing the frog. Now she was the frog. Celeste was the snake.

She wanted to do as Mr. Nichols said, but the voice seemed to be taking over her ability to think and act. It took an enormous act of will to keep her eyes away from those terrible, beautiful eyes. "There's a good boy. I will find you and talk to your parents about all the things I can do for you."

Grace did not answer her.

"Or perhaps you have no parents? Is there no one with you, my dear? Why do you not answer me?"

Grace said nothing, trying with all her might to make her hands pull the lid to the box closed. Yet still, she stood there.

"Have you no manners that you do not answer me?" Now Celeste's voice turned deadly cold. "It is a dangerous thing to be alone in a vast cavern. Unimaginable horrors lurk in every corner. Loathsome, slimy creatures, hideous things will sneak up on you and follow you, sniffing your trail, haunting you wherever you go for as long as you live. They will find you in the night when you think you are safe. Look around you well and to your own safety."

Fear welled up in Grace. She had an almost overwhelming desire to look around her. But she didn't. Nevertheless, she could not close the Alabaster Box.

"Did you not hear me?" this time the voice rose in a terrible shriek. "There are horrors you cannot imagine ready to devour you! Quick, while you can. They are nearly upon you, you idiot child!"

Idiot child. It sounded like Mrs. Swathmore screaming at her. Something about that shriek gave Grace the strength she needed. Gritting her teeth, exercising all of her willpower, she forced her hands to close the lid to the Alabaster Box without once looking away from it.

The voice ceased. The eyes were gone. All was silent. Shaking all over, Grace stood for a long time bracing herself against the alabaster cairn, collecting her thoughts. She didn't know how long she stood there before she picked up the blanket holding the wooden box. Holding it at arm's length, she carefully walked back over the alabaster bridge, handing it to Mr. Nichols.

"No, I can't take it, Grace," he said. "The magic is too strong. It was especially designed to keep me out. I have placed a terrible burden on you, and you have done well. Nobody could have done better. We will put the box in your saddlebag and be away from here with all due haste."

"I looked, Mr. Nichols. I didn't mean to, but I looked into her eyes," Grace sobbed.

"I know, dear," he said gently. "But think how brave you were. You didn't look again. That was the hardest of all. And in spite of everything, you have the crystal."

"Can she see us?" asked Grace.

"Not now. Only when you saw her reflection."

"But she said…"

"She wasn't telling the truth. She could see you, but she doesn't know who you are or anything about you. She was trying to gather you into her power so you would tell her all you know. Then she could protect the crystal for herself. She wanted you to look around so she could see the cave through your eyes, but you overcame her. She has no idea who you are and how you got here."

"But she saw me at the hotel," said Grace.

"I doubt she paid any attention, but even if she did, she has nothing to go on. When she saw you in the reflection of the box, she thought you were a boy. She won't think of the pretty girl in the new dress seen at the hotel in passing."

"She said I looked ordinary." Grace felt her face go hot with the memory of Celeste's unkind words.

"She had no interest in children then. That explains the loophole in the magic, too. She didn't consider children. She'll pay more attention now," said Mr. Nichols. "My job is to get you back to St. Louis where you will be safely tucked away with your grandparents. You've done a great thing, Grace, greater than you know. It is not finished, for the box will need to be opened one day. But it is enough for now. The stars will sing tonight! The crystal is no longer in her hands. I must find a way to protect it from her. But first, to St. Louis. It would not do for us to run into Celeste and she may make haste to come check on her crystal."

Chapter 19

To St. Louis

Getting to St. Louis took much longer than it took to get to the Alabaster Cavern. Mr. Nichols was determined that there should be no trail that could possibly lead to Grace, so they didn't take the most direct route. But what a glorious adventure they had!

They stayed in a Niukonska village. They traveled by canoe up the Arkansas River for a day, meeting the horses on the opposite side. (Grace was never sure how the horses got there.) Once they huddled at the bottom of a dry riverbed as a tornado swept overhead, crashing trees all around them. They watched wild ponies race across the plains and rode a steamboat down the Missouri, reaching Kansas City from the north.

Chapter 19

It was hard to tell Patches and Song of the Wind goodbye before they left to board the steamboat. Mr. Nichols said Patches was not a tame pony and wanted to return to the prairie. He said Song of the Wind would go where he wished and come when he was needed.

As she patted Patches, he nuzzled her with his soft muzzle. Telling Song of the Wind good-bye was another matter. There was something stern about him that made her feel shy. She turned to him, "Good-bye, and thank you for everything," she said awkwardly. Song of the Wind reached his long neck toward her, ears pointing forward. When he nickered softly, putting his soft muzzle against her cheek, she abandoned fear, throwing her arms around his neck.

Once they were in Kansas City, Grace and Old Shep waited while Mr. Nichols went for their things. He brought her a very old dress she could wear until they got to the hotel where Rosy waited to help her with a bath in the big tub. This time she got to sleep in the featherbed.

They traveled by stagecoach to St. Louis. The boxes with the crystal rode in a small carpetbag that Mr. Nichols bought just for that purpose. Grace carried it, even when the stagecoach driver wanted to put it up on top with the other baggage. Old Shep rode in the coach with them, so well behaved that none of the other passengers objected.

"Now Grace," Mr. Nichols said when they arrived in St. Louis, "this is a great thing you have taken on yourself. The crystal will be safe as long as it is with you and as long as you keep it in the carpetbag. Under no circumstance are you to open the carpetbag or the boxes inside. The carpetbag must not be carried by anyone but you, because you are the one who opened the Alabaster Box. Not even your Grandpa and Grandma should touch it. If there is ever a time that you cannot promise this, you must let me know immediately.

"There is a great deal I must still learn about the magic. When I do, I shall return for it."

"How will I find you?" she asked.

"You just have to call me," he said. "I will come. Or send Old Shep. He can always find me."

When they arrived at the Willis home, there was great joy that Grace had been found. Mr. Nichols stayed overnight, leaving early the next morning.

"How can we ever repay you for your kindness?" Grandpa Willis asked as they stood on the front porch to see him off.

"Such things are not to be repaid, they are a gift to be received," said Mr. Nichols. "But there is a great favor you could do me. I have asked Grace to watch over something important. I want to make sure it will be safe and undisturbed."

"Put it on the top shelf of your closet, Grace, dear," said Grandma Willis. "Nobody will bother it there."

So Grace put the carpetbag on the top shelf of her closet where it remained. Grandma Willis made gingerbread cookies and Grandpa and Grandma Rhoads came to celebrate. She showed Grandma Rhoads that she still had the lace hand-kerchief.

As time passed, she was too busy going to school and growing up to think about the crystal very much. She was happy to be back where things were familiar and comfortable, where she could sink into a featherbed at night, far away from the horrors of the Swathmore dugout and the grief that dogged her on the Santa Fe Trail.

But somebody else thought of the crystal.

Chapter 20

THE MYSTERIOUS SHEPHERD

Celeste sat at the dressing table in an elegant hotel room in San Francisco looking in the mirror. "I am the most beautiful woman the world has ever known," she said it out loud, smiling a self-satisfied smile. All the so-called beauties of the West she'd first met when she visited Kansas City ten years ago, were beginning to look like old hags. *But I will never age*, she thought.

Removing the stopper from a crystal vial, she dabbed her temples, behind her ears and wrists as one might apply perfume. This was no perfume. The vial contained life-giving water from the sixth crystal. She'd been using it for hundreds of years. She became a mere mortal to have this water for herself. But what did it matter? With water from the seven crystals she lived as an Immortal. She returned the vial to the velvet, silk-lined, box that accompanied her everywhere, locking it shut.

Admiring her reflection in the mirror from behind a lacy fan, Celeste frowned. She was getting ready to attend a masked ball. Masked balls were out of style in Europe, but this was the frontier. *How am I to be the toast of a masked ball if nobody can see my face? I must be seen if I am to attract the attention of that adventurer from Paris.*

In the society circles of San Francisco, tongues were wagging about a man known only as C. Shepherd. He was said to be an adventurer who came from vast wealth. According to the best gossip, he was as at home with kings and queens in Europe as he was around the campfires of American Indian tribes in America. Rumor had it that Shepherd came west to hunt buffalo to add to his collection of trophies collected in Africa and India. Now he was visiting San Francisco.

Celeste hadn't heard of him when she was last in Paris. *Shepherd isn't a French name. If he is French his name ought to be Berger*, she thought. *Wonder what the C. stands for? He probably has homes all over the world. That will suit me fine.*

Ainsley, who had been her companion ten years ago, was long since gone. If asked, he would have said he was worn out by Celeste's constant, unreasonable demands. She said he was getting old and boring. So Celeste was on the lookout for an interesting male companion with lots of money to spend on her. Money wasn't enough, though. He had to be sufficiently good looking to provide a suitable background for her astonishing beauty when they appeared in public. It was no good being on the arm of an ugly man. People would say it was just the stark contrast, not her beauty that caught their attention.

Celeste dressed as an Egyptian princess for the masked ball. More than three thousand years ago she was in the royal courts of ancient Egypt where everyone admired her. She knew exactly what to wear. She had a white gown made for the occasion. It was not unlike one of the simple gowns worn by Nefertiti, the Egyptian queen. She had a wide collar made with pearls, a simple hair cover, and a golden cloak to complete her attire.

That night, shortly after she arrived for the ball, Celeste spotted a man wearing the costume of a simple shepherd. *C. Shepherd, of course!* He'd dressed to match his name. He was taller than anyone else in the room. As balls often did, this one began with a Grand March. The host and hostess led couples around the room in time to music. Celeste kept an eye on the tall man in the shepherd's costume as her suitably handsome escort led her through the March.

They paraded by twos up the center of the room, women splitting off to the left and men going right. Celeste enjoyed this part. It was a way to be seen by everyone else in the ballroom. As the women came around and met the men, they passed by, making an inner circle. Celeste held her head aloof, as regal as any Egyptian princess. The march ended and the dancing began. She wasn't short of admirers wanting to get on her dance card, but the shepherd was not among them.

She took a break, positioning herself near where the shepherd was standing. He didn't show her any attention. So she sent her escort off on an errand and began coughing. The shepherd brought her a cup of punch.

"Nefertiti, I presume," he said. The voice was vaguely familiar, though she was sure they had not met. His facemask covered him so well that there was little to identify him, but there had been whispers all evening. He had to be C. Shepherd.

Giving him her most dazzling smile—her mask didn't hide her smile—she demurely took a sip of punch and thanked him.

"How is it that we have not met?" she asked, coughing again ever so slightly for effect.

"Oh, but we have," he said. A quadrille was announced. The shepherd bowed politely. "May I have the pleasure of this dance? That is, if you are sufficiently recovered from your cough."

"No, we haven't met. And yes, I enjoy dancing." Celeste said, as the dancers moved into formation. "I'm sure we haven't met. I don't think I would forget you." She gave him her most charming smile. Unfortunately, batting her eyelashes was of no use behind a mask.

The quadrille was a dance where couples came together and whirled around, joining hands with other partners and coming back together again. So their conversation went on as they passed each other in the dance.

"Can you not guess?" the shepherd asked, twirling her around.

"You are Mr. Shepherd of whom much as been spoken," said Celeste in a teasing voice as she glided back to him.

"But that does not answer my question," he replied when they met again. "Can you not guess where we have met?"

"All my efforts fail," Celeste sighed a pouting sigh. "I'm afraid you're going to have to refresh my memory." The dance separated them so she had to wait until he came back around.

"You are Celeste and you are much older than you look," he said, stopping in the middle of the dance floor. The other dancers whirled by.

She, too, stopped. "Who are you to speak to a lady in such a pertinent manner," she said, only slightly annoyed. *He is flirting with me*. It was going exactly as she intended.

"Is the truth so hard to bear?" asked the shepherd. He did not sound as if he were flirting.

Suddenly dreadful reality dawned on her. "C'lestin!" she sputtered in fury, stamping her foot. Right there in the middle of the dance floor she began pounding him on the chest with both fists. "How dare you!" He caught her wrists and flipped her around so that her arms were crossed, gliding from the dance floor in time to the music. She was powerless to hit him.

"A most curious dance step," remarked a man dressed as George Washington, who was standing along the side of the ballroom. "Must be one of those primitive frontier dances."

"Yes," said his companion, dressed as Martha Washington. "Something suitable around campfires; perhaps before an attack on settlers."

"Most irregular," said a haughty woman dressed as a fairy.

"Perhaps something new from the continent?" asked a man dressed as an Indian raj. "I wonder how they did that?" He began trying to duplicate the step. "I'd like to try it."

"How dare you come here and ruin my evening," hissed Celeste.

"I thought you found me charming," he said. "You went to a great deal of trouble to attract my attention, faking that cough. Besides, I was invited, too. Why shouldn't I enjoy an evening?

Especially when it gives me the opportunity to dance with my twin sister. Shall we step outside for a quiet word?"

"Is this where I must endure a tedious sermon about repenting and changing my ways?" her voice was cold as steel. "Or am I allowed the luxury of waiting another two hundred years?"

C'lestin said nothing, maneuvering her toward doors that opened to a garden.

"You're ahead of schedule. Every five hundred years is more than enough," Celeste said bitterly.

"Really, Celeste, is it worth it?" asked C'lestin. "How boring to go from one party to the next with admirers fawning over you, year after year, century after century. I see the boredom in your eyes. Surely there must be some thread of goodness left in you, calling you to a better life." They stepped out into a large garden. Celeste quit fighting.

"Don't ask me to be sentimental about our past, C'lestin. I am not. I was the Keeper of the Crystals, yes. You were to assist me. After all, I was born before you. What a useless part we were given to play in the life of the earth," she scoffed. "Yet you will persist in trying to play it."

C'elestin shook his head sadly, removing his mask. "We had it in our charge to heal and preserve the earth. How can a life of being beautiful replace a life of such vast importance?"

"Don't be dreary, C'lestin. I'm not interested in duty and honor. Earth is doomed. It has been since it was created. You know that, as well as I do. What a colossal waste it would have been to use the crystals to patch up the earth. The very sun we orbit will burn out. What is there to save?"

C'lestin smiled, a sad smile. "The beauty of Mother Earth, the glory of her seas, and mountains, and rivers, and skies for as long as her sun shall last. Her infinite variety of animals, and fish, and birds. The love that binds all living things together."

"Love is an antiquated concept," scoffed Celeste.

"And you, Celeste. You are worth saving," said C'lestin.

"I think I'm going to be sick." She mocked.

"And ruin that lovely costume? I think not. Who would want to dance with you then?"

Celeste ignored him. "I have used the crystals for my own enjoyment. Why not? What I want is important to me. I get what I want. Nefertiti herself said I far surpassed her beauty. Helen of Troy was nothing compared to me. I am the woman of legends, the most beautiful woman who has ever lived on this planet. I walk in and out of history, influencing the powerful, changing the destiny of men."

"And when it comes to an end?" C'lestine asked.

"Oh, please! I have millions of years to think about that."

"And if you didn't?"

"But I do," sneered Celeste. "There is yet another crystal bound in magic so powerful that even you cannot claim it, brother dearest," she said with disdain. "And if anyone else should try, there is no place they can hide it that I will not know. Must we go over this again? You were defeated from the beginning."

"No, my dear twin," said C'lestine. "You were defeated from the beginning. There is more than one way to repair the world. But you are not so easily repaired. You could choose, even now, to undo your magic and restore this last crystal to its intended purpose."

"You, above all others, know that I resigned my magical powers when I became mortal," said Celeste sarcastically.

"You have always had power over the crystals. You worked that out when you were an Immortal. You can undo the magic binding the Last Crystal. It isn't too late. If you do, you will grow old and die as mortals do. But you will die anyway, Celeste. Eventually you'll run out of water from the crystals. But if you return the crystal, you'll die knowing that you have left the Earth a better place. The water from that crystal could do so much good."

"Not in a hundred, million years," jeered Celeste.

"You may not have even a hundred years," said C'lestine.

'Why do you keep annoying me?" asked Celeste. "I haven't budged in a million years, yet you keep showing up and spoiling my fun."

"Love never quits trying," said C'lestin.

"Not that again. Next thing you'll be asking me to weep because there's been a landslide in Siberia or some rare reptile has just vanished from history. Go away and let me enjoy myself."

"I leave you to your dance," he said. With that, he turned on his heel and walked out through the garden, disappointing many a woman at the dance who had her heart set on the wealthy adventurer in the shepherd costume. Little did they know that the Immortal C'lestine had riches they couldn't imagine. But they did not include a country estate near Paris and he would never decorate a home with animal trophies. Ever. He pulled his shepherd's cloak around him, walking quietly out into the night. There were tears in his eyes.

Celeste's evening was ruined. A visiting Count from Germany, dressed as a matador wearing a flashy red cape, declared her the most beautiful woman he had ever met on three continents. He proposed on the spot. Even this triumph could not salvage the evening.

There was something about the way C'lestin said, "You may not have a hundred years," that troubled her. The more she thought about it, the more disturbed Celeste became. *Of course! He was behind that boy finding the Alabaster Box so long ago.* Yet nobody had opened the golden box. It had been at least ten years. The crystal was still safe. The boy couldn't have taken the box without her knowing it. Or could he? She hadn't counted on a child. It disrupted the magic, perhaps more than she'd supposed. *It is high time I find that boy.* He would be much older by now, if he were still alive. That would be an advantage. She'd met few men who were not susceptible to her charms. There was work to do. It was time she checked on the crystal again.

But Celeste was distracted. It so happened that the Count, who had proposed at the ball, was wealthy beyond her wildest dreams. A small delay in checking on the crystal was of little consequence, particularly since it was so well protected. After all, she had safely kept six crystals. There was no reason to believe she could not keep the Last Crystal. To live well, it was necessary to have a source of income. The Count was pleasant company, too. So it was not wasted time to secure his affection. Anyway, there was quite a lot of water left in the vial from the sixth crystal.

Chapter 21

GRACE FORGETS

Grace didn't mean to forget Mr. Nichols and the carpetbag. But eventually the memory began to fade. She moved the carpetbag up to the attic to make room for new hats on the top shelf of her closet. After that, it went completely from her mind. Had she thought about it, she wouldn't have worried. Grandpa and Grandma Willis never went to the attic anymore. They were too unsteady on their feet. What safer place could there be?

She grew up to be a very good artist and a school teacher. She married David Henry, a young man who was a geologist, surveyor, and cartographer (or map maker). After they were married he was hired to help map the land west of the Rocky Mountains. The crystal stayed forgotten up in the attic of Grandpa and Grandma

Willis's big house while Grace and her husband explored the country all the way from New Mexico to Canada and from west of the Rockies to the Pacific Ocean. The truth is, Grace had become more of an adventurer than she realized. They slept under the stars and in a tent when the weather was bad. Grace made sketches of plants and animals they encountered. David surveyed the land and made maps. Later, when their travels were over, they published a very big and important book on the American West. It was full of interesting maps and pictures Grace painted from her sketches.

Grace was especially proud of one particular map that she kept for herself. It marked their way from Albuquerque, New Mexico across the mountains to the ocean, up the coast to the Columbia River and the Cascade Mountains, then on to Mt. Rainier. From there it followed along the eastern edge of the Columbia Plateau to the Great Salt Lake and down again along the western side of the Rocky Mountains, ending back in Albuquerque. It wasn't a real map like the others they made. It was as she imagined the map might have looked thousands of years ago. She was inspired by the fact that the land is constantly changing. Rivers change courses over time, mountains are sculpted by ice, wind, and earthquakes. Coastlines change as salt water and wind eat away at the sandy banks and wetlands along the shore. So the map had to be guesswork based on David's best hunches as a geologist.

Along the borders she painted tiny pictures of some of the animals and plants they saw.

The idea for the map came to her when she found an old parchment scroll among David Henry's things. "Are you saving this for something special?" she asked.

"I didn't know it was there," he said. "I have no idea where it came from."

"Well, it's just the thing for a commemorative map for our baby," said Grace.

When a little boy was born, they named him James and took him along on their travels. They had completed their map-making expedition, when a baby girl was born. Because she looked so much like her mother from the moment she was born, they named the new baby Grace.

They rented a house just outside Albuquerque, New Mexico. It had plenty of room for them to work on their book about the American West and for James and his baby sister to play.

On James's eighth birthday something curious happened. A black and white dog came bounding up the steps of their big porch and jumped right into James's arms.

"Why he looks just like your Old Shep!" said David Henry. "I thought he disappeared years ago. He couldn't possibly have lived this long."

"He disappeared right after we were married," said Grace. "Grandma Willis said he was gone one day. They never knew what happened to him."

The dog turned to her, wagging all over in recognition. "Why, you are Old Shep! How can this be?" Grace had almost forgotten how extraordinary Old Shep was.

Old Shep's arrival made Grace think of somebody she hadn't seen in years. She was pretty sure that particular somebody was the one responsible for Old Shep finding them. The carpetbag came to mind, too, and her promise to keep it with her. She hadn't kept the promise. She had a sinking feeling as she remembered.

Grace put off dealing with it, though. The memory of the Alabaster Cavern and getting the crystal had taken on a dream-like quality over the years. She wasn't entirely sure that it wasn't just a dream. But there was the carpetbag. Why had Mr. Nichols asked her to keep it? And there was Old Shep. It was impossible that a dog could live that long, yet Old Shep was undeniably the dog she'd known as a girl.

Grace was torn. Grandpa Willis died before she and David left for their expedition to the West. A Civil War gripped the nation in their absence from St. Louis. Grandma faced it alone, writing that she had become a member of The Ladies Aid Society helping to care for Union soldiers and freed slaves. They followed war news when they were able to get the mail or a newspaper. Grandpa Rhodes wrote regularly, too, keeping them posted on war news from the countryside. He reported that Missouri was a divided state with neighbor against neighbor. They usually got a packet of letters at a time. But they were generally in the wilderness, away from the affairs of the world around them.

Now Grandpa and Grandma Rhoads were gone. Grandma Willis wanted to meet the children. But going back to St. Louis meant facing the memory of that carpetbag.

Then David surprised her. "The book is done. Grandma Willis has been asking us to come back and live with her. Why not? I want James and Grace to know their Grandpa and Grandma Henry, too. There's nothing keeping us here. Train travel makes it an easy journey now. It's time we went home."

Grace knew he was right. So she agreed even though it left knots in her stomach. They packed up and took the train from Albuquerque, New Mexico to Kansas City, Missouri. From there they took a steam boat to St. Louis.

Grace looked out the window as the train made its way across the desert-like lands between Albuquerque and Kansas City, remembering. Had it all really happened? Even the trip in the covered wagon along the Santa Fe Trail and the awful months with the Swathmores seemed far away. Why should she feel guilty? It was such a long, long time ago.

Chapter 22

ANOTHER SET OF TWINS

One afternoon Celeste stretched out on her satin sheets for a nap. She was as gloriously happy as she could be. Everything was going her way. The Count was ready to return to Europe where Celeste could appear before kings and queens. A whole generation of royalty was growing up without having had the opportunity to admire her. *Life is good when you are young and beautiful,* she thought. It was then that she heard voices.

There were two. She could faintly see two dirty faces looking at her from the Alabaster Box that held the Last Crystal. One was an unshaven man wearing a cowboy hat. The other was a woman with long stringy hair. She was wearing a cowboy hat, too, and a man's shirt.

"Lookie here, Ruby. Somebody's been in this here cave before us," said the man. "Hidin' treasure from the look of it."

"Reckon why they didn't take this here pretty box?" asked Ruby.

"Reckon it had somethin' more valuable in it, like gold," said the man.

These are no children. They should be dead. Celeste sat upright in bed. *So why are they still alive? Anyone opening my Alabaster Box and threatening the crystal should die instantly— except for the child. Something isn't working.* It was a terribly unsettling thought.

As it happened an infamous set of outlaw twins had just discovered Alabaster Cavern by chance. After robbing a bank in Dodge City, they were running from a very persistent lawman. They rode south, eventually coming across the canyon. It looked like a good place to hole up for a few weeks. In exploring, they stumbled upon the entrance to the cavern. It wasn't long before they entered the crystal room and discovered the black alabaster cairn. It still held the Black Alabaster Box where Grace left it years ago.

The twins were Ruby and Junior Swathmore, all grown up and two of the meanest outlaws ever. They terrorized Northern Texas, Oklahoma Territory, and Kansas, robbing stagecoaches and banks for the fun of it. They never passed a schoolhouse without setting it on fire, turned cattle loose from their pens for the heck of it, and shot holes in water tanks just for pleasure. Their pictures were in practically every post office from southern Kansas to Texas with a sign that read, WANTED, DEAD OR ALIVE.

Ruby peered into the lid of the Black Alabaster Box, "You can see yourself in this here lid, Junior." She took off her hat. "I'm lookin' real good," she said, tossing her head.

"Whoa, this thing is scary," said Junior. "You don't look that good, Ruby. That ain't your reflection you're lookin' at. Reckon we've found us a magic box with a genie in it, like that there lamp that good for nothin' girl used to tell us about when we was kids."

"Before she run off, you mean," said Ruby.

"Yeah, the story about Aladdin. Grace could tell a right good story. I'll say that for her," said Junior.

"She could cook better'n Mamma, too, when Pa would let her," said Ruby. "Reckon why she wanted to go and run off like that? She left us havin' to eat mushy corncakes, crunchy beans, and scorched 'possum even when Pa was away. That is 'til Myrtle got old enough to cook."

"Say there, Genie Lady. How many wishes do we get?" asked Junior, peering into the face that now filled the lid.

Celeste could see them clearly at last. She pronounced the spell that should have stopped them dead in their tracks when they opened the box.

"Who is this who dares to open my Alabaster Box? Know you not that it is forbidden?" she demanded. It didn't work.

"Know you not? What kind of gibberish is she talkin', Junior?" asked Ruby.

"Shut up. I think it's genie talk," said Junior, tipping his hat to Celeste. "Hey, Genie Lady. No need to get all riled up. All we want is three wishes and you can go back to sleep."

Celeste tried her soft, sweet voice on them. "Oh, but you see, I don't grant wishes. The boxes are mine. I can't allow you to take them. That would be stealing."

"Don't that beat all, Junior?" Ruby broke into a fit of laughter. "You got this all wrong, Genie Lady. Thievin' is what we do best. You might say it's our profession."

Celeste tried another tactic, this time using a firm voice. "I am the one for whom the boxes are intended. If you take what is mine, you will die. The boxes are protected by magic more powerful than anything you can imagine. Close the lid and leave the boxes inside. Walk away while you can or be cursed and die!"

"What boxes?" asked Ruby. "Ain't nothin' in this box but you, and you ain't doin' nothin' for nobody. You a genie or ain't you? Let's see you strut your stuff. I wish I was the prettiest lady in the whole wide world. What can you do about that?"

"That position is already taken," retorted Celeste, instantly furious with herself for letting Ruby get her goat.

"Don't throw away our wishes!" ordered Junior, giving Ruby a shove with his elbow. "I wish I had the fastest horse in the West and they was enough banks to keep me stealin' gold for the next ten years."

"Foul! That's two wishes," said Ruby. "Besides, she still ain't doin' nothin'. I can't even see myself in the lid anymore."

"Well, you ain't any prettier than you was, that's for sure," said Junior. He pointed his gun at the lid of the box. "Get on with the wishes before I shoot your lovely face off, Genie Lady."

"You ain't, *haven't* been listening," said Celeste in a fury. She was starting to get rattled. These two simpletons were not responding the way they should. "I cannot grant your wishes," she said sweetly to Junior, ignoring Ruby. "The boxes are mine. Close the lid and you will live. I could use a smart, handsome man like you, Junior. I know hundreds of banks that haven't ever been robbed. They are filled with vast piles of gold, just waiting for someone clever enough to get them."

Chapter 22

"You hear that Ruby? More banks! Full of gold. Genie Lady could use a handsome feller like me." Junior grinned and yawned without covering his mouth. He was suddenly starting to feel sleepy. There was something about the lady's eyes that made him want to go to sleep.

Insolent Clod, Celeste thought. But she used her most charming voice, "There's so much we could do together with your brains and my beauty."

"She don't know you, that's fer sure," grumbled Ruby. "He's as stupid as he is ugly, Genie Lady. Dumb as a post. Put that in your pipe and smoke it. You ain't as smart as you think you are. You'd better shut up all that fancy talk. Me and Junior would as soon shoot you as look at you."

Celeste lost her patience and screamed, "Touch anything else and you will die. Run where you want to, you can't escape me. Wherever you go I will see you and I will find you. There is no place on this earth you can hide from me. Now take your hands off of my boxes!"

"Now Genie Lady, don't go gettin' your feathers in a fluff," yawned Junior. "We done told you there ain't any boxes inside this here black rock box. What do you take us fer anyway?"

"She ain't no genie," snorted Ruby. "You're still as stupid as you ever was."

"And you're still as ugly as sin," retorted Junior.

"Close that danged lid and shut off her wind," demanded Ruby. "I'm tired of hearing her yappin' like a wounded coyote. We can fetch a pretty penny for this here box if we keep her inside." The lid closed. Celeste could see no more of the twins.

She flew into action. Had that boy outwitted her all those years ago and actually taken the crystal? How did he know the exact words of the spell? There were some big questions she'd failed to ask. There was no time to waste. She was so upset she didn't even look in the mirror before she rang for the maid. "Tell Count Gerhardt that I must have a rail ticket from San Francisco to Dodge City, Kansas immediately. And tell him I prefer the southern route through Los Angeles. He can come with me or not as he chooses. He will need to hire a private car in any case. I cannot possibly ride in coach with the common riff-raff."

A lavish private car was attached to the train from San Fransisco when it departed the next afternoon. The private car was joined to the new rail service from L.A. to Chicago. Celeste and the Count were aboard. Celeste didn't notice, but when the train stopped in Albuquerque, New Mexico, a family of four boarded. Their black and white dog was comfortably resting in a cage in the baggage car. It wasn't until the train stopped in Dodge City, where the private car was uncoupled from the train, that Celeste saw a face that she had been unable to erase from her mind.

Chapter 22

She had just stepped out of the private car and was standing on the platform when Little Gracie, now three-years-old and the image of her mother, decided to put on her brother's cap. Little Gracie looked out the window and waved as the train pulled away from the station.

"The face. That's the face I saw," Celeste screamed. But not even Count Gerhardt and a platform full of people running after it, could stop the train. Before she could do or say anything else three faces peered at her from the Alabaster Box.

Chapter 23

THE EMPTY BOX

"Lookie here, ain't that the dangest thing you ever saw?" asked Junior, grinning at her.

"It's yours for ten dollars in gold coin," said Ruby.

"That's a mighty pretty face, but you're askin' way too much money," said a man, the third of three faces Celeste could see. "Five gold dollars. That's my best offer."

"Why you'll make that much back the first time you bring it out," said Junior. "If you work it right, you can get the lady to talk. She can talk up a storm, when she has a mind to, that's fer sure."

Celeste didn't feel like talking. She looked at them because she couldn't keep from looking.

It was the way the magic worked. If any of the boxes were opened, she could see and her face could be seen. It was supposed to protect the boxes. It wasn't meant to let stupid, churlish, nincompoops gawk at her.

The box closed.

"You are not well, *meine Liebste*," said the Count taking Celeste's arm.

"I have a headache," said Celeste. "A terrible roaring headache."

"It is the noise and smoke from the trains," said the Count. "We must get you to our car where you can rest."

It took Celeste much longer to get to the Alabaster Cavern than she intended. The man looking at the box was a snake oil salesman who traveled all over selling his cure-all medicines and fake magic tricks. Junior and Ruby sold him the Alabaster Box for seven gold dollars. He made a lot of money selling tickets to let people open the box and see Celeste's reflection. Unfortunately for her, she couldn't do anything about it. Having given up her magical powers when she became mortal, she had to rely on the magic she set in motion from the beginning. So every time the snake oil salesman opened the box, she had to stop what she was doing and look at whoever was looking in whether or not she wanted to. She didn't have to say anything, but she had to look. She could count on a severe headache every time.

The day after the snake oil salesman bought it, the box was opened and shut constantly all day. Celeste had one long, terrible headache and had to go to bed.

Once the spell wore off that was the end of it. Nobody knows what the salesman did with the box. But Celeste was disabled for nearly a month. For three weeks she stayed in the private car, eating very little, staring into space, and complaining of headaches. As the spell wore off, she could think more clearly. By the fourth week she was ready to travel.

The Count insisted on going with her to the Alabaster Cavern. He had no idea what they were looking for, but he was worried about her. They set out for the Cavern with a party of hired gunmen just in case they ran into trouble. It didn't take long for her to see the appalling truth for herself. The crystal was gone without a trace.

There was an exciting moment or two when Ruby spotted them coming up on the entrance to the Cavern. She wanted to shoot first and ask questions later. But Junior was more practical this time. Besides, his distance vision was better than hers. He recognized Celeste from her reflection in the box and demanded to know about the banks piled full of gold.

The Count was baffled, but a good sport. He'd never met an actual outlaw and found the experience highly entertaining. Ruby kept him occupied by showing him the finer features of her pistols and how fast she could draw and shoot. She was so fast that none of the hired gunmen wanted to challenge her. In fact, one of them was so terrified of her that he resigned on the spot and high tailed it back to Dodge City alone.

Meanwhile, Junior struck up a deal with Celeste. She hired the twins to find the girl who'd waved to her from the train.

Celeste spoke privately to Junior. Her orders were very specific. "Find her and get rid of her. She has a wooden box with gold hinges that belongs to me. I want it back. You are not to touch it. Clear the way. I will come get it. If you dare try to open it, I'll skin you alive. Don't think I can't find you, because I can, just like I found you here. No distractions that might land you in jail, either. I'll pay you more money than you ever dreamed about. As far as I am concerned, you can rob every bank between here and California when you're done."

"You got yourself a deal, Genie-Lady!" said Junior, extending his hand to shake on it. Then in a stage whisper, he said, "Tell you what, if you can get rid of that fat man you brought with you, I reckon you and I can have some real good times!"

Celeste limply shook his hand. "My name is Celeste, not Genie-Lady," she said imperiously. "When I have the box I require, we shall see about the good times." As soon as he let go of

her hand she rubbed it fiercely with her handkerchief.

"Hot diggity!" said Junior.

"I'll tell you what," said Ruby, eyeing the
Count. "I never met any genuine royalty before.
Any time you want to learn how to draw and
shoot, I'll be glad to teach you. Free of charge.
No strings attached."

"I believe that you and Junior have work to
do," said Celeste icily.

"This box, it must be most precious," said
the Count.

"It is a family heirloom, stolen from me years
ago," Celeste lied.

Chapter 24

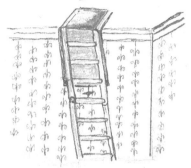

THE SECRET IN THE ATTIC

Once they were back in St. Louis, Grace put off going up to the attic. She didn't think about it very often. When she did, she made all kinds of excuses. After all, if the crystal were that important, Mr. Nichols would have come for it a long time ago. Still, she worried that she hadn't kept her promise to keep it safe. *Except it was safe and it is still safe*, she told herself. *If I'd carried it around all over the West it wouldn't have been safe. I don't think he intended me to do that.* Except he had said she must promise to keep it with her. She hadn't.

Months passed. Grandma Willis, who was very old and frail, died, leaving her big old house to Grace. They were grateful that they'd returned in time to be with her. David said that they shouldn't ever sell. There were too many happy memories built into that house. Grace agreed. She had given up one big old house in St. Louis when the family left for Kansas City. She couldn't bear to think of giving up this one.

It looked as if they were comfortably situated in St. Louis for good until one morning when little Gracie explored the attic. That changed everything.

David was away at the library. Grace was in the kitchen making a piecrust when suddenly a loud thud came from upstairs. It was the fold down steps, an invention Grandpa Willis had built to make it easy to reach the attic. *How many times must I tell that James to leave those stairs alone?* She sighed. He was under strict orders never to go into the attic. He'd never disobeyed. But he couldn't resist pulling on the cord that let the steps down and using them as a climbing toy. *I really must have David put a shorter cord on those steps so he can't reach it,* she thought. She could hear James jumping from the ladder. *Of course he'd be doing that right when I'm in the middle of something,* she thought, patting the dough out onto the breadboard.

She was rolling the piecrust out into a nice round circle, when she realized that it was awfully quiet upstairs. Little Gracie was nowhere to be seen. Wiping her hands, she left her work unfinished and started upstairs. "James! Not the ladder again."

Chapter 24

James stood at the bottom of the stairs looking up. "I told her not to go up there, Mamma," he said. "But she went anyway."

***

Celeste was in a hotel room in Chicago when it happened. She saw a face looking at her and laughing. It was the little girl she'd seen waving at her from the train. She'd obviously opened the wooden box. Her face was just like the face of the boy she'd seen so long ago, but much younger and cleaner. The little girl laughed, opening and shutting the box, calling, "Hello! I see you."

"Look James! See the lady in the box?" the little girl called.

This girl must not get away, Celeste thought. "Hello my dear," she said in her most charming voice when the box opened again. "Do you like my pretty box?"

The girl laughed, nodded her head and closed the box, cutting Celeste off. It opened again. There were giggles.

"Oh, please don't shut the box. If you do, we can't talk to each other," Celeste said sweetly. The little girl looked at her with a serious expression on her face.

"Another box!" the girl said, pointing. "It's a golden box."

"Oh no. You mustn't open the other box. It is my box. I shall be very cross with you if you open it. This box is more fun."

The girl seemed to be thinking it over.

"Look at me, dear. What a pretty little girl you are. Such lovely eyes. We can play together if you like."

The little girl nodded her head. She looked right into her eyes, just what Celeste wanted.

"My name is Celeste," she said in a soft, soothing, hypnotic voice. "What's your name?"

The girl just looked at her, wide-eyed.

"If we're going to play together, I need to know your name. Let's see, you must be Donna and you live in Dodge City." Celeste knew next to nothing about children, but she'd seen ridiculous adults who doted on them play guessing games. It was worth a try.

"No," said the girl, shaking her head. "Guess!"

"Oh dear. I was wrong. I'll guess again. Let's see, you must be Clara and you live in Chicago," said Celeste.

"No-o-o," said the girl, laughing.

"Karen in Kansas City?" asked Celeste.

"No, no, no!" the girl laughed.

"Not wrong again!" said Celeste in a mock pout. "One more guess. You are Irene in Indianapolis."

"I'm not Irene in Indianapolis," the little girl shrieked with laughter.

"I'll never guess. I give up. You are too smart for me." Celeste let out a great, mock sigh.

"My name is Gracie Henry and I live in St. Louis." The little girl yawned.

Celeste could hear footsteps and a boy calling, "Mamma says come down right now, Gracie."

A woman screamed, "Gracie, close that box immediately!" The little girl disappeared from view. The lid on the box was closed. Celeste smiled a wicked smile. *No matter. I have all I need to know*. Calling her maid, she commanded, "Tell the Count that we must catch the next train to St. Louis. We have no time to lose. And I want a telegraph message sent to Stella Ruth in care of the Dodge City telegraph office."

Stella Ruth was really Ruby Swathmore. It was the code name they'd agreed on for getting messages back and forth. The twins were so well known they didn't dare appear together. Ruby did all the work that required a public appearance. It was the only time she wore a dress and bonnet, something she detested. But it worked. Nobody ever recognized her.

"Any messages for Stella Ruth?" she asked the clerk at the telegraph office.

"Afternoon, Miz Ruth," said the clerk. He knew her. Ruby checked twice a week. "Happens I do have a message for you."

Ruby looked at the big picture of herself with Junior posted on the wall of the telegraph office while she waited for the clerk. It wasn't a good picture. She was tempted to have one taken and sent to the sheriff just so they'd have a more flattering picture to post.

"Here we are," said the clerk. "Want me to read it to you?"

Ruby couldn't read or write so he always read any letters or telegraph messages sent to her.

"Taking train from Chicago tomorrow morning. Found the girl. Meet me at Planter's Hotel, St. Louis as soon as possible. C."

"Reckon you'll want a train ticket to St. Louis, then," said the clerk.

"Sure thing," said Ruby. "Make it two. Mr. Ruth will be makin' the trip with me. Our darlin' daughter ran off, God bless her. She's been found."

"I'm so happy for you," said the clerk.

By the time Junior and Ruby arrived in St. Louis, Celete had located the Henry home. "It belonged to the Willis family," she told them. "Apparently they were very prominent in St. Louis so it is in a very nice part of the city. You will have to be careful. You can't go riding up on horseback waving pistols. You'll have the law on you before you can find the right street. Hire a buggy. Junior, you need to wear a suit. The Count will take you out to buy one. And you need another dress, Ruby. That one looks like," she paused. "I don't have words for it." Then, thinking it over, she added. "You are both going to have to have baths."

"I ain't takin' no bath. I'll catch my death," said Junior in disgust.

"Me neither," said Ruby, putting her foot down.

"Okay. That's fine," Celeste said coolly. "I will find someone else to do it. Never mind about good times and banks without number."

"Ah heck!" said Ruby. "I hate getting all gussied up. You can't wear six-shooters over a fancy dress and all those petticoats. Do I have to take a bath?"

"You can put a gun in your purse," said Celeste firmly. "And yes. You have to take a bath."

"Purse?" Ruby sat down hard on one the parlor chairs in the rooms Celeste and the Count had taken. "Not a purse. Next thing you'll want to put my hair in curls." She moaned, putting her feet up on a tea table.

"What a novel idea," said Celeste. "Come with me. I'm paying you good money for this. We'd better do it right." With that, she rang for her lady's maid, instructing her to round up a team of hotel maids and meet her in Ruby's room. She personally marched Ruby back to her own unused bath chamber. "Here," she said to the attendant. "See if you can do anything with her. I'll admit there's not much to work with."

To Ruby, she said very quietly, "No squawking and no back talk." Even so, it took three of them to get her in the tub and four to hold her down for a shampoo. Gallons of water were spilled on the floor. Nobody complained. Celeste paid them well.

When Ruby returned to Celeste's suite, bathed and hair piled up in curls, she was stunningly pretty. "Well lookie here, Junior," she said, looking in the mirror in Celeste's sitting room. "I reckon she is a genie."

"You don't look half bad, Ruby," said Junior. "What do you think of these fancy duds?" He'd been the victim of a bath, haircut, and shave. Now he wore a fashionable three-piece suit and stove pipe hat. "Reckon we'd better get out of here. We've got work to do."

Chapter 25

LITTLE GRACIE FALLS ASLEEP

By the time Grace got up the ladder, little Gracie was telling Celeste her name and where she lived. Grace screamed. Grabbing the box, she closed it. Something like an electric shock went through her hand and arm when she touched it. Gathering Gracie into her arms, she cried, "Oh Gracie, what have I done?" But Gracie didn't answer. She was fast asleep, head slumped over onto her mother's chest. "Mr. Nichols, help! Whatever are we to do? This is all my fault." Grace sobbed, rocking Gracie back and forth. "Mr. Nichols, please come quickly. This is all my fault." *What if he has forgotten me?* "Old Shep!" she called, "go find Mr. Nichols."

"What is it Mamma?" called James from below. "Will Gracie die?"

Calming herself, Grace said, "Oh no, James. Come here, up where we are." She asked him to return the box to the carpetbag and close it. The box had been wrapped in a shawl. "Don't touch the box, dear, wrap the shawl around it first." Something told her that now she shouldn't touch it again, even the carpetbag. The shock was like a warning. But James was a child. Mr. Nichols said that the spell binding the boxes had no power over a child. "Little Gracie is just sleepy. You go down the steps first and hold them steady. I'll bring her."

"Is she alright, Mamma?" he asked.

"Just sleepy. She'll be fine." Grace wasn't at all sure she would. *I felt the power of Celeste's eyes once. How long did Gracie look into her eyes?* Once down the ladder she took Gracie downstairs, laying her on the parlor sofa. "We'll let her sleep here where we can keep an eye on her. I'm sorry I was so frantic, James. It's just that I promised to look after that carpetbag and not ever let anyone get into it. It isn't your fault."

At just that moment, the doorbell rang.

"Telegram, Mam," said a boy from the telegraph office.

Thanking him, she opened the message. "Let Gracie sleep. There by dinnertime. If you haven't told David about contents of carpetbag, tell him now. C. Nichols."

Chapter 25

So when David Henry came home shortly afterward, James was sent out to play in the back yard. By the time Mr. Nichols arrived, Grace had told David the whole story.

"There is no time to lose," said Mr. Nichols as he walked in the front door. Old Shep was right behind him. "You must leave immediately. Bring the carpetbag. I know a farm where you will be safe for the present. The owner will be away for the year."

"I don't want to be involved in this business anymore," wept Grace. "I was a child. I didn't know what I was promising. It's too much to ask now that I have a family."

"So it is with promises. They are more easily made than kept," sighed Mr. Nichols. "Unfortunately, you can't give the crystal back. And Gracie's life will be forfeit if Celeste finds her. It's part of the wicked spell. I have been studying it since the day you opened the Alabaster Box. I've been out of time and mind. I know a bit more about it now than I did then. The spell couldn't harm you when you were a child, and it can't harm Gracie unless she opens the gold casket that holds the crystal. Fortunately, she didn't. But obviously she has come under Celeste's power. Celeste can harm her and through her, get to the crystal. We must get her and the crystal away from here. Celeste was on the morning train from Chicago. She will know exactly who you are and where to find Gracie in a matter of hours."

"I can't take that bag with me. You see what happened even with it hidden upstairs," sobbed Grace.

David was already collecting their working gear. "It doesn't sound like you can back out now, Grace."

"But we can't possibly get ready to go so quickly. There must be some way to stall her," cried Grace.

"We've lived simply before," David said calmly. He was already piling maps, papers, compass, square, rulers, ink and water colors in a suitcase. "We can do it again. Quickly now, get some things packed up for the children and for us. I'll take care of our working materials. We will leave everything else here. We will return when it's safe."

"Can't you do something, Mr. Nichols? You must have some kind of power over all of this," Grace said, wiping her eyes.

"Would that I could," he said. "All I can do is aid you in what you must do. And for now, you must hurry."

"Why can't we just leave the hateful thing here and let her have it?" Grace asked.

"Grace, you know we can't do that," said David.

Grace sighed, going up the stairs.

Within the hour they loaded a few bags in the carriage Mr. Nichols had waiting for them.

As they were leaving the house, Mr. Nichols removed the large map that Grace had made from where it hung on the wall. "Just leave it!" Grace said. "It isn't a real map anyway. It can stay."

"There is more to this map than you know," he said, rolling it up.

"Here, you'll want this, too, Grace," said David. He reached up and took a smaller frame that hung on the wall where the map had been. Pulling the frame apart he handed Grace the lace handkerchief Grandma Rhoads had given her.

Gracie was still asleep. Mr. Nichols said it would wear off with no harmful effect except for Celeste's influence over her. "We'll just have to keep her away from the crystal and away from Celeste," he said.

James knew that they weren't going on a holiday. But nobody told him why they had to leave. He felt pretty sure it had to do with the carpetbag. Mr. Nichols asked him to carry it. It was his fault for letting Gracie climb the stairs. He felt terribly guilty.

Just outside St. Louis, Mr. Nichols took them to a large barn that stood alone in a hay field. They spent the night there, sleeping on the hay. James slept next to Old Shep. He thought it was great fun sleeping in a barn and not having to have a bath and get into pajamas.

Gracie woke up the next morning. "Where did the lady go?" she asked. "I want to play with the lady."

"Give the lace handkerchief to her," said Mr. Nichols. "A lot of love has gone into that handkerchief. Love is what she needs most right now."

David already had it in hand. "I was thinking that myself," he said, handing it to Gracie. Picking her up, he gave her a kiss on the cheek. "I love you, Gracie."

Little Gracie clutched the handkerchief like a lifeline, clinging to her Daddy.

"James," said Mr. Nichols privately. "We will have to keep the carpetbag away from Gracie. She's going to want to open it again. We can't let that happen. You're the only one who can take care of the bag now. There are some things only a child can do."

"Yes Sir," said James. "But why, Sir? Will the bag make her go to sleep again?"

"I'm afraid so," said Mr. Nichols. Then he explained as much as he thought James needed to know about what was happening.

James thought for a minute. "So if she opens the box the wicked lady can see her and make her go to sleep again. And she'll know how to find us."

"That's right," said Mr. Nichols. "You must be in charge of the carpetbag."

"So it wasn't all my fault," said James, relieved.

There was a buggy stored in the barn. They left the carriage and took it. "This will keep them off the trail for awhile," said Mr. Nichols. "And it will be less conspicuous."

"Them?" asked David.

"Celeste has had the best scouts money can buy searching for you for nearly a year. We'll have to stay ahead of them."

About the time Mr. Nichols and the Henry family began looking for a suitable place to spend their second night on the road, Junior and Ruby were pulling up in front of Grandma Willis's old house in their hired buggy.

Nobody was at home. Ruby twirled her parasol and looked out from the porch while behind her back, Junior made quick work of picking the lock to the front door.

"They ain't gone fer good, somebody's been makin' a pie," said Ruby.

They did a thorough search of the house from top to bottom and the stable behind. "Horse and buggy ain't gone," said Junior. There was no box matching Celeste's description to be found.

"Well lookie here," said Ruby, pausing on their way back through the house. She held up a picture of Grandpa and Grandma Willis with Grace, taken when she was twelve-years old.

"It's Grace Willis! Reckon how she got here?" asked Junior.

"Hot diggity!" yelled Ruby, "We'll get her this time."

"We'll get her back for Mamma and Celeste can pay us for doing it!" said Junior. "That's puttin' butter on the bacon."

"We'd better start asking the neighbors where our dear 'cousin' Grace and her family have got off to," said Ruby.

Chapter 26

VISITORS FROM THE PAST

Little Gracie was sound asleep in the upstairs bedroom across the hall from James. The lace handkerchief was in one hand. James buttoned up his pajamas and crawled into bed waiting for his mother to tuck him in.

When Grace tucked him into bed she gave him a kiss, just like she always did. "I love you James," she said. "And I'm proud of you. Don't ever imagine any of this was your fault. I should have taken better care of the carpetbag. You're doing a much better job than I did."

David was right behind her, slipping into the room to blow out the candle. He gently laid a big hand on James's forehead for just a moment and whispered, "Sleep well, son."

With the children safely in bed, Grace let out a sigh of relief. All day she had been uneasy. She tried working at her drawing desk. She and David were finishing a new book about the geography of the West, a project making use of all their old notes. It was also one that they could do from almost anywhere, which was fortunate since they had been living on the run for the past two years.

She couldn't focus on her work. She got up, pacing back and forth to the kitchen, unable to relax.

"How about a cup of tea before we turn in," said David. "I'll put the kettle on."

"I have the jitters," said Grace. "It feels like something awful is about to happen."

"Maybe you are worrying too much," said David.

"It's so hard to live like this, not knowing from one minute to the next," said Grace.

"We've always managed to stay ahead of danger," said David. "But you can call for Mr. Nichols if you're worried, or send Old Shep to get him."

"Five moves in two years. It is too hard," said Grace. "Too many narrow escapes. How long must we live this way?"

Just as David put the kettle on somebody knocked on the kitchen door. It was late for neighbors to stop by, but it must be somebody they knew or Old Shep would be making a fuss. "I'll get it," he said.

"This where Grace Willis lives?" a man asked. "We knew her when we was kids."

David looked at Grace. They were thinking the same thing. How would anybody know to ask for Grace Willis? They were known as David and Grace Brown. Every time they moved, they changed names.

"We was just passin' through. Reckon we'd like to come in." It was Ruby Swathmore, pushing her way past David. "You remember us, Grace? Our Ma and Pa took you in when you was an orphan."

Grace remembered. She remembered why she was an orphan, too. "Come in. We were just putting on the kettle. How about a cup of tea?"

"Heck, why not for old times sake," said Junior, grinning at Ruby. The two were dressed like anyone you'd meet in town. Ruby's dress was a bit rumpled and she wore cowboy boots underneath. Her bonnet hung behind her back. They both had an un-scrubbed look about them, though, despite the clean clothes.

"So tell me about the family," said Grace, after introducing them to David. They sat at the kitchen table.

"Well, Ma's dead," said Ruby, brushing stringy hair out of her face. "Pa set his-self up with a trading post on the Canadian River after that trapper and his Injun wife was burned out. Made a right good business of it. Good thing the fire didn't get most of the inventory."

Probably got the trading post the way he got our wagon, thought Grace. She was apprehensive.

"Things was too hard on Ma's nerves after you run off. The baby died," said Ruby. "She never did take to that baby, but it hit her hard when he died. She never did too good at the trading post. Reckon it was your fault for running off like that. She couldn't find good help after you was gone. Course there was Myrtle, but it wasn't the same. By the time she was much good, Myrtle run off to go to school."

"I'm sorry to hear about the baby and your mother," said Grace. "Is your father still alive?"

"He's too mean to die," said Junior. "Don't reckon I know. We ain't checked up on him in years. Us two decided to strike out on our own. Ain't been back since."

"Pa took out that strap one time too many," said Ruby. "We high tailed it out of there. I ain't never goin' back."

"So what are you doing with yourselves these days?" The kettle was singing. Grace got up to make tea. "Mr. Nichols! Wherever you are, we need help!" She breathed the words. There was something terribly wrong with Ruby and Junior showing up out of nowhere, asking for her. How could they possibly know? And why would they want to find her?

"Don't you want to know about Otis and Myrtle first?" asked Ruby. "You always favored them two."

"I'd love to hear about them. They were really sweet children," said Grace, setting the teapot on the table.

"Not like Junior and me!" snickered Ruby. "We was always bad. Nobody was better at bein' bad than us two."

"Where are Otis and Myrtle now?" David asked politely. Grace could see that he was uneasy, too.

"Don't reckon I know where they live," said Junior. "Myrtle done got herself ed-jee-cated. She was an old maid school teacher, last I heard tell. Someplace over in Oklahoma. Reckon she'll be doin' it forever. Can't think as anybody would want to marry the likes of her."

"Not everybody wants to get married," said David matter-of-factly.

"Otis done become a preacher," said Ruby. "Got his-self a regular circuit. Rides around preachin' the gospel to the Cherokee. They made him an honorary member of the tribe. Can't think why he'd want to go and waste his time on Injuns."

"Leastwise it keeps him from preachin' at us," grinned Junior.

"Maybe he and the Cherokee don't find it a waste of time," said David. "I imagine it would be interesting to work with the Cherokee. A person could learn a lot."

"They have a long history and their own alphabet. Has he learned to read their language?" Grace asked as she set out cups and saucers. It was clear that Junior and Ruby hadn't changed. They were just bigger editions of two rotten kids.

"Can't stand to be around either one of 'em," said Junior, looking at Grace. "Think they're better 'n anybody else like some others I could mention."

"So where are you two living now?" asked David, keeping his voice calm and even.

Grace's mind raced ahead. How could they protect the children if Junior and Ruby turned on them? *Where are you Mr. Nichols?* They never had a gun in the house. They hadn't even carried a gun when they were out West mapping the country back in the years before James and Grace were born. Their guide carried a gun, but only for hunting.

"We got us a place in Oklahoma. Ain't too far from the old dugout," said Ruby.

"So do you ranch or farm?" asked David politely.

"Nah. You might say we work with the law," said Junior, winking at Ruby slyly. He looked just like Mr. Swathmore. It gave Grace the chills.

"That's a good one, Junior! What he means is, we keep the law in work." Ruby cackled with laughter.

"Would you like some pie?" asked Grace. They were in trouble. If only they could stall Ruby and Junior there might be a chance of Mr. Nichols getting there in time. She could tell that David was trying to figure out how to draw them off.

"You used to make mighty good apple dumplin's before you run off," said Ruby. "Ma didn't like you makin' 'em. Showed her up."

"I remember how much you liked them," said Grace. "And I remember how you used to love to hear the story of Aladdin and his wonderful lamp."

"That there was always my favorite," said Ruby. She sounded almost wistful.

"We didn't hear you drive up," said David. "In fact, I'm surprised the dog wasn't barking. He usually raises a fuss."

"They was a big black and white dog like the one we used to have standin' out there," said Junior. "The one that ran off with you, Grace. Remember Old Shep? This 'un took one look at us and high tailed it off somewheres. Must not of liked Ruby's looks."

"Must not of liked the looks of you," retorted Ruby.

He recognized them. He went for Mr. Nichols, thought Grace. She wasn't able to explain it, but she understood that Old Shep knew where to find Mr. Nichols no matter how far away he was.

"How thoughtless of me," said David. "You must have horses that need to be tended to. It is late to be traveling. You must stay the night here. Maybe we should put the horses in the barn, then have our pie." He stood, starting for the door.

He's trying to get them away from the children, thought Grace. *Whatever they want, it can't be good.*

"Nah, sit down. We got our mind on pie," snickered Ruby.

"Shoot, I figured you was still makin' pies when I saw that pie crust you left out in St. Louis!" said Junior. "Ran right off and left it."

"You ought not to have said that, Junior," scolded Ruby. "You always was a dumb cuss. Never could keep your yapper shut."

That was it. They were working for Celeste. "I have a cherry pie. Let me get it," Grace said calmly, going to the pantry. "Mr. Nichols, help us. I don't know how long we can hold them off," she whispered as she took the pie from the shelf. "Hurry, Old Shep."

"Don't bother cuttin' that pie," said Junior as Grace set it out on the table.

"You got this a commin'," Ruby said, pulling a gun from her boot.

*****

James woke up suddenly and couldn't go back to sleep. There was a sliver of moonlight pooling on the floor of his bedroom. The bedroom was long and narrow with a window on one side opposite the bed. It looked out over the roof of the front porch. The dresser next to the window was a dark shadow against the wall. The clothes closet door wasn't quite shut. It cast a shadow over the door to his room.

The carpetbag holding the crystal was on the top shelf of his closet. Mamma counted on him to carry the carpetbag every time they moved. While Daddy distracted Gracie, Mamma held a chair for him while he put the carpetbag on the top shelf of his bedroom closet. "We will leave it here until the right time," she said. "We will know." She said that every time they moved.

Suddenly, silently, Mr. Nichols was there, leaning over him, making a heart shape on his forehead with his left index finger. "Shhh. James Henry, I've come for you. Little Gracie is with me. Quickly now. Get the carpetbag. I'll get the map."

Nobody had to tell James it was the right time. Mr. Nichols had given him the signal. It meant he and Gracie were to go even if Mamma and Daddy weren't there. Leaping out of bed, he pulled on his clothes, pushed a chair up to the closet, and got the carpetbag.

"I'll go first. You hand Gracie down to me," Mr. Nichols whispered. He stepped from the window, dropping to the roof of the porch below.

James leaned out the window, holding Gracie. Mr. Nichols took her in his arms. Then he reached up and helped James. Holding Gracie, Mr. Nichols jumped from the roof of the porch to the ground. He set Gracie down next to Old Shep, who waited silently. Holding up both hands, he motioned for James to jump.

Taking a deep breath, James shut his eyes. He jumped, holding on to the carpetbag.

In a flash Mr. Nichols lifted James and Gracie onto the back of a horse who waited with Old Shep. Leaping on behind, he wrapped a warm blanket around the two of them. Gracie gripped the lace handkerchief. James held the carpetbag and the map.

"Move away from the house, Old Shep, and keep watch," said Mr. Nichols. "There's nothing we can do for the others." Suddenly Old Shep was no longer there.

The horse sprang to a gallop. "We must fly, Song of the Wind!" said Mr. Nichols. "Everything depends on speed! Don't look back, lad, and don't let Gracie look." As they sped along the dirt road from the house, the sound of a terrible explosion came from behind. It shook the very ground around them.

They were going so fast it was hard to tell, but it seemed to James that they really were flying. The stars were clear and bright, brighter than he had ever seen them. Below, the tops of the trees were dark. Then they were in a village. Mr. Nichols said it was a Chumash village. Somebody gave them hot soup and wrapped them in blankets warmed by a fire. Mr. Nichols said Gracie must stay in the village for her own safety. The box in the carpetbag has put Gracie in danger. Nobody can find her here.

The people in the village call Mr. Nichols something else. James isn't sure. It is a different language. It is all like a dream, like a dream he is in and watching at the same time. James wasn't sure about time, how long it took to get there, how long they were there. Maybe it was days. Maybe it was weeks.

An old woman with long gray hair speaks to him. James can't understand. Mr. Nichols says, "She is called Malipuyaut. She is a very good and wise woman, James. She is the village shaman. That is like being a doctor. Your Grandpa Willis was a doctor. She takes care of people. She's telling you that Gracie will be loved. She will care for her as if she were her own child. She knows Gracie will miss your Mamma and Daddy terribly and she will miss you. Malipuyaut will never let Gracie forget you. We will come to visit her sometimes."

James wanted to scream and cry out, "No! No, you can't have her. She's my sister. She's my family." But he didn't. He opened his mouth, but the scream wouldn't come.

Malipuyaut gave him a shell, a red abalone shell. He could almost see himself reflected in the inside it was so shiny. Mr. Nichols said, "She wants you to have this. She wants you to always remember."

"What of Mamma and Daddy? They will miss Gracie," he protested.

"It is so very sad, James," Mr. Nichols said, "Your Mamma and Daddy can't come where Gracie is or where you will be. I was able to save you and Gracie. I could not save them. I am so sorry they aren't with us. They love you so very much."

James leaned his head against Mr. Nichols, sobbing until there were no more tears to cry. "Seems like that carpetbag is more important than anybody," he said.

"I know, James. Your Mamma felt that way sometimes. Maybe that's why she didn't want to keep it with her when she grew up." Mr. Nichols sounded very sad. They sat together on the grass watching little Gracie frolic with other children. Malipuyaut looked at James and smiled. She called. Gracie came running, arms out wide to hug James. Then Malipuyaut took Gracie by the hand. They walked away together.

Chapter 27

THE BEAUTIFUL HILLS

Grace Willis Henry sat up, stretching. She hadn't had such a good sleep since she couldn't remember when. Looking up she saw light dancing through the leaves of a graceful, old elm tree. If light could be said to sing, this light was singing the most joyful song she had ever heard.

David Henry was beside her, yawning and stretching. "How long have I been asleep?"

"It feels like ages," said Grace. "Where are the children?"

"Mr. Nichols got them before the fire reached the back of the house. They're going to be fine," yawned David. "I'll miss getting to see them grow up, though."

"So he got there in time," said Grace. "It won't be so very long, will it, before we see them again?"

"I don't think so," said David, stepping out from under the elm and into the surrounding meadow. "This is a beautiful spot. It reminds me of that high meadow on Mt. Rainier. Remember how we sat there one afternoon before James was born? There were wild flowers everywhere. And we saw a pika gathering flowers for her haystack. You made a sketch of her for James's map."

"And the air was so fresh," said Grace. "The colors here are more vivid, though, don't you think?"

"I wonder why they renamed the mountain?" said David. "I suppose all the explorers thought they should. It was like there was nothing before the Europeans came. Vancouver is the one who named it, long before our time. But Tahoma was such a pretty name."

"Tahoma, the mountain that was God," said Grace. "I suppose it seemed that way to the early people. The volcanoes must have been terrifying. A volcano would terrify me, too."

"I don't think we have to be worried about anything here," said David dreamily. He took Grace's hand and pulled her out from under the tree and into the light.

"And David, look how blue the sky is. Remember when we stayed in the Chumash village on the coast? That was the bluest sky I ever saw before now. The people were so kind."

"Gracie will be safe there, among the Chumash," said David. "That's where Mr. Nichols is taking her. She will be safe from Celeste there."

"Do you remember racing dolphins in the plank boats?" asked Grace. "Maybe Gracie will get to do that. I think she'd like to see dolphins."

"Those were wonderful days," said David.

"What ever happened to the condor feather they gave us? That was a very special gift," said Grace.

A man and woman stood at the top of a low, grass-covered hill nearby. Radiant light shone around them. They waved. "Is that you, Grace? Come with us. David, too!" the woman called.

Hand in hand Grace and David walked into the light at the top of the hill. There was a gentle breeze. Wild flowers danced and bowed as the breeze skipped through them. They were breath-takingly beautiful in the splendor of the light. As they got closer Grace dropped David's hand and ran, throwing herself into the arms of her mother. "You're all grown up and such a lovely woman, too," said Mamma. "I'm so proud of you."

"We've been waiting for you," said Daddy. "There is someone else who wants to see you, David."

Climbing up the hill from the other side, through the joyful light, was David's father. His mother was close behind. There were Grandpa and Grandma Willis, and Grandpa and Grandma Rhoads. David's grandparents were there, too, and a host of relatives, so many Grace and David could hardly remember. "Come on with us," said Grandpa Willis. "We've so much catching up to do."

"But the children. They'll miss us," said Grace.

"Of course they will," said Grandma Willis. "But they will be just fine. Before you know it, they'll be here too. Why, it seems hardly any time since we left. Now here you are." She put her arms around Grace.

"Welcome, Grace. I'll bet you don't remember me," a tall man who looked vaguely familiar stretched out his hand in greeting. "I'm Sid Johnson."

"Sid Johnson!" exclaimed Grace. "Yes, how could I forget you, Sid?" Then looking around at the cloud of faces, she said, "It seems like just about everybody I ever loved is here."

"That's one of the best things," said Grandpa Willis. "There's no need to rush, either. We have all the time in the world."

Chapter 28

A TIN BOX

A singed Ruby and Junior reported to Celeste. The farmhouse where the "Brown" family were living had been set afire with all members of the family inside.

"How can you be sure they are dead?" Celeste asked skeptically.

"Oh they're dead, alright," said Junior. "First thing we did was draw a circle around the house with gunpowder. Laced the sides of the house with kerosene, too. Then we marched ourselves right up to the front door all friendly like."

"Back door. Back door, Junior. Get your facts straight," said Ruby.

"What about the girl, that little girl? I gave specific instructions," Celeste demanded.

"You should have seen that place light up," said Junior. "Whoopie! That there was a fire to remember. Better 'n the one Pa set when he burned down that tradin' post. That's sayin' somethin', too."

"Nobody left that house," said Ruby. "It burnt to the ground right before our eyes. There weren't no way to escape. Couldn't even find their dog. They's dead for sure. No doubt about it."

"So how's about our money and the names of those banks waitin' to be robbed, like you promised?" asked Junior.

"What about the box?" demanded Celeste. "That was the most important thing."

"What are you going on about a box for?" asked Ruby. "Weren't no box to be found."

The truth is, they'd forgotten about the box in their eagerness to have revenge on Grace Willis.

"Of all the incompetent, STUPID, blundering buffoons," shrieked Celeste, her face turning red. "The box was the whole point. I haven't met anybody so dumb in a million years! Get out of my sight before I call the sheriff and turn you in for the reward."

"Reckon you don't want to turn yourself in, too," said Junior, cool as a cucumber.

"Don't try to outsmart me. You can't. You have nothing from me in writing," Celeste said in a low, hideous voice. "And if you did, you couldn't read it. Who do you think the sheriff will believe? You, with your faces all over every post station and railroad stop or me, with my Count and respectable life?"

"She's got a point there, Junior," said Ruby. "Reckon she's meaner than we are. That there's somethin' to respect. Best be on our way and leave her to herself. Sorry about that there box, Miss. Sure appreciate the chance you gave us to even the score with Grace Willis. Reckon you can keep that there dress you dolled me up in and this 'un to boot. Danged uncomfortable."

"I'm keepin' my togs. I like the look of 'em," said Junior. "They suits a man like me."

"Get out of here!" screamed Celeste, shaking in rage.

Ruby and Junior left before Ruby had a chance to change out of her dress and with no payment for their evil deeds. Celeste went with a team charged with sifting through the ashes of the house. The boxes were bound by magic. They wouldn't burn. But, the only box they found was a burn-scorched tin box with her name on it. When Celeste opened it she found a note: "Dearest Sister, It is out of your reach. It isn't too late to change your mind. Love no end, C'lestin."

"You have not heard the last of this, C'lestin," she shrieked.

When she returned to the hotel in St. Louis where they had lived for the past two years, the Count was there. He had been away on business.

"*Meine Liebste,*" he said. "You do not look so well. I hope the headaches do not trouble you again."

Celeste threw a sofa pillow at him.

Chapter 29

JAMES REMEMBERS

James awoke in a warm bed under a pile of soft blankets, remembering things. He remembered when Mr. Nichols first came to their house in St. Louis. They had to leave. Every time he came to see them, they moved to a new house far away. It had something to do with Gracie and the carpetbag. It had to be kept hidden from her. And the whole family had to stay hidden from somebody who wanted Gracie and the carpetbag.

Sometimes Gracie would stop in the middle of what she was doing. "Where is the box? I want to see the pretty lady in the box," she'd say.

Mamma always said, "That was in St. Louis, dear. We aren't in St. Louis now." Then she would get an old lace handkerchief and give it to little Gracie to hold. "You are loved, Gracie.

Hold on to love," she'd say, wrapping Gracie in her arms. Sometimes James came and put his arms around them both. Daddy did too. They'd have a great big family hug.

Some days Gracie would ask the same question three or four times. "Where's the box?" She always wanted to go up into the attic, no matter where they were. The idea never left her mind.

James wondered what would happen if she found the carpetbag and opened the box again. Mamma said they weren't going to let that happen. James figured that if Gracie opened the box she would be at the mercy of the lady who put the spell on her.

A tear made its way down his cheek, splashing on to the pillow. He couldn't keep from crying when he thought about the saddest night of all. It was the last time he saw Mamma and Daddy. He wondered if he'd ever quit crying when he thought of them.

"Come have some breakfast, James," called a lady. "Mr. Nichols is already at the table." James sat up in bed, trying to think where he was.

He remembered then. They came late last night. Mr. Nichols introduced him to the kind lady. He put the carpetbag on the top shelf of the closet before he went to bed.

Now he couldn't remember her name. He was so tired last night. He was embarrassed to say he didn't remember. "I hope you had a good night's sleep," she said pleasantly, leaving the two of them to their breakfast.

Over pancakes with blackberry syrup, Mr. Nichols told him about how his mother broke the spell holding the Last Crystal. "You see, when your mother opened the Alabaster Box, it became her task to keep the crystal with her," he said. "I had to study long and hard to find out how to finish the work she began. Don't ever blame her for what has happened. The fact is, she did what nobody else could do. It was a very brave thing. She broke the spell holding the Alabaster Box, so the crystal was safe with her as long as she didn't open the remaining boxes. The power of that dark magic weighed on her the rest of her life."

"If she'd kept it with her like she promised, would it have undone the magic?" asked James.

"Maybe. We'll never know," said Mr. Nichols, finishing his pancakes. "The magic must be undone carefully. The Last Crystal is locked by cruelty greater than you can imagine. It can only be undone by the opposite of great cruelty. That is great kindness. Undoing the magic will be a perilous quest."

"Will little Gracie have to do it? She opened the wooden box."

"Not your sister Gracie. When she came under Celeste's spell she was too damaged to ever face her again. Sometimes the best you can do is stay away from what it is that hurts you. Gracie will not undo the magic, but someone very like her will."

"I will," said James. He meant it, too.

Mr. Nichols stood, putting his arms around James, giving him a big hug. "You are a fine lad, James. The kindness of your offer is priceless. But you have done your part. Now you must wait and see. You and I can assist. Think what we've already done. We have protected Gracie. Celeste cannot harm her now. The crystal is safe. When the time is right, the crystal will be waiting to do its part to repair and heal the world."

"How can it do that?" asked James.

"The water inside that crystal is the water that was here when the world was created. It is healing, life-giving water. Unfortunately, people do not always respect and care for the Earth, our home. Where people have left the earth in ruin, a few drops of that water could make it right again."

"I wish we could use the crystal now," said James. "Then maybe Gracie could come back with me."

"Well, James, thankfully, there is more than one way to repair the world. Who knows? Perhaps all the kind things we do that seem small in themselves add up to more than all the good that can be done by one crystal and the water it holds. When you plant a garden, or return a fallen bird's nest to a tree; when you love, when you forgive, you are repairing the world."

Anticipating him, James said, "We'll know when the time is right."

"Yes, James. I think we will," said Mr. Nichols. "Now, if you've finished with breakfast, there's somebody outside waiting to see you."

It was Old Shep, so happy he was wagging all over. James, who had wondered if he could ever laugh again, found himself laughing out loud as Old Shep pounced on him, knocking him down on the soft, green lawn. He had no idea what would happen next, where he would go, who he would live with, when he would see Gracie again; but James knew that it was going to come out right. Mamma once told him that awful bad things can happen. There's no stopping them. But wonderful things happen, too. You have to decide if you're going to accept the adventure you're given or lock yourself up in misery.

James picked himself up off the grass. "Come on, Old Shep," he said. "Let's see where Mr. Nichols is going to take us next."

ABOUT THE AUTHOR

Frances Schoonmaker and her two brothers were reared on a farm in Western Oklahoma, not far from where The Black Alabaster Box takes place. Her parents were farmers and schoolteachers. She became an elementary school teacher, too. Later she was a professor at Teachers College, Columbia University in New York until her retirement. Now "Miss Fran," as the neighborhood children know her, lives in Baltimore, Maryland with her daughter, granddaughter, two adorable, but contentious cats, and a hamster who remains above the fray. She has always been fascinated by the history of the Great American Westward Migration and by books that create imaginative worlds. In The Black Alabaster Box, she creates a world that makes room for both fact and fancy.

ABOUT THE BOOK

"It's incredibly hard to please a whole class of fifth graders when choosing a text to read aloud, but I'm pretty sure that the The Black Alabaster Box did just that. Not only did the students learn a great deal about westward expansion and life on the trail, but they were swept up right along with the intriguing characters in their startling adventures within a setting that teetered back and forth between fantasy and historical fiction. Many students wanted to find out more about the Santa Fe Trail and surprised me with facts and information from that time period that they had sought out on their own. As we read, we laughed and we cried, we were constantly left in suspense, and above all, we couldn't wait to read on each day!"

–Katie Schmidt, Rodgers Forge Elementary School, Baltimore, MD

CPSIA information can be obtained
at www.ICGtesting.com
Printed in the USA
BVHW04s2108220918
527808BV00009B/5/P